The Woman in the Cistern

A San Amaro Mystery

Marnie J Ross

The Woman in the Cistern

A San Amaro Mystery

Marnie J Ross

MEERSCHAUM PRESS

Editor: Beth Dorward

Cover: Bart Hopkins

ISBN 979-8-9944565-0-7 Paperback

Other books in the San Amaro Mystery Series

Death in the Baja
Death in the Kitchen

Praise for Death in the Baja:

C.B.W. - 5 Stars

As someone accustomed to a menu of non-fiction and historical fiction, I was somewhat skeptical that a mystery novel would hold my attention. The backdrop of this story is a place with which I am very familiar. So, despite some misgivings, I decided to give it a try. I found the premise to be engaging and the details realistic. The many twists, turns, and red herrings provided by MJR kept me turning the pages; suspecting almost everyone; and, dead certain I knew exactly "who dun it,"—until the very end. I couldn't have been more blindsided! I was left smiling and shaking my head at just how dead wrong I had been. A delightful surprise and a wonderful distraction from my normal "sugarless" reading diet. Well done, MJR! Looking forward to the San Amaro, Baja sequel.

Amazon Customer – 5 Stars – Wonderfully Surprised

I have to be honest in saying I bought this to read as the author is the wife of a childhood friend and I wanted to support her. From the first few pages I was hooked. I am the type of reader that when I love a book I don't stop until I'm finished. Needless to say I did nothing but read for two days. I loved the development of the characters, and the anticipation of what the next page may present. I simply loved the book. Great job for first endeavor and I cant wait for the next book. This is a great read.

Praise for Death in the Kitchen:

Eljay - 5 Stars

Ross has come to writing later in life, and brings her knowledge to the pages of small town Mexico. The second of the series is even better than the first.

Editorial Reviews – Death in the Kitchen

A genuinely engrossing mystery. Ross's ability to create compelling, multidimensional characters and a gripping mystery driven by surprising revelations make this novel a standout. Featuring excellent characters, an intense investigation, and a satisfying ending, Death in the Kitchen has everything I look for in a murder mystery. *Readers' Favorites (5 Stars)*

Ross skillfully builds suspense, taking readers on a captivating journey to uncover the killer. The intricate plot twists and turns keep readers engaged and guessing until the very end. This powerful read is sure to leave a lasting impression on readers. *US Review of Books (Recommended)*

To Fisher, Willa, Denae, Laine, and James
You give me hope for the future!

Contents

"He whom the flame of jealousy encompasses, turns at last, like the scorpion, the poisoned sting against himself."

Friedrich Nietzsche —*Thus Spake Zarathustra*

Chapter One – Fifteen Years Ago

A bass line vibrated through Heather's body—a pulsing rhythm that seemed to sync with her heartbeat—as she and her friends crossed the raised walkway toward the dance club. As they approached, the familiar lyrics of *"Stayin' Alive"* by the Bee Gees became clearer, sending a thrill of nostalgia through her, the bass reverberating in her chest.

Heather couldn't help but nod along to the beat, her movements instinctive, and soon she was singing the chorus with unabashed joy. Her friends joined in, their off-key harmonies mingling with laughter as they neared the entrance of the throbbing club. Tonight promised to be unforgettable.

With partners left behind at home, the four women embraced a rare and cherished girls' night out: dinner, a few drinks, and dancing until their feet ached. Because it was a celebration, they had stepped up their wardrobes from their usual shorts and T-shirts.

Once a ballerina with a small reputation, Mona retained her lithe figure and sported a classic, simple black dress, flats, and chunky Mexican silver jewelry. Kim, the tallest of the group at five-ten, had paired silver capris with a white and silver scoop-neck silk top.

Laurie, the most athletic, looked like she'd just left the golf club in a lime-green sleeveless golf shirt and matching green golf skort with a blue geometric pattern. Apart from a sports watch, Laurie wore no accoutrements. Heather had taken the celebratory aspect of the evening to an extreme, wearing a glittery, New Year's Eve-worthy dress in silver and gold lame with matching flats, a necklace, and a pair of earrings comprised of a fine gold chain attached to a stud.

They had savored a delicious meal at *El Delfin*—The Dolphin—just across the Malecon from the vibrant Cha-Cha Club. The occasion was Mona's fiftieth birthday, a milestone that demanded celebration.

Though their friendships were relatively new, they had quickly become close, bonded by the shared experience of living as expatriates in San Amaro, Baja. Heather and Kim were permanent residents, while Mona and Laurie split their time between Mexico and the United States.

The club was housed in a large, bright-white building perched on one of the mini-mountain-like hills at the northeast end of the Malecon. It was reached by a set of metal stairs and a metal walkway over a small inlet of water separating the street from the club. It resembled a cubist's vision of a lion crouching on a rocky hillock.

The building's only adornment was *Cha-Cha Club,* painted in blue stylized block letters on its front. In the tiny fishing village of San Amaro, the Cha-Cha Club was the hottest ticket in town.

The final notes of "*Stayin' Alive"* reverberated in their ears as Mona held the club door open for her friends, the throbbing energy of the club washing over them. Gloria Gaynor's empowering anthem "I

Will Survive" began to play, and Mona's eyes lit up. Grabbing Heather's arm, she pulled her toward the dance floor. "C'mon, let's dance. I love this song!"

Kim and Laurie joined them, and they danced and sang along with blissful abandon, their spirits soaring with the music.

From across the sea of merrymakers, a group of four men noticed the lively women. The tallest, a square-jawed, handsome blond man in his early fifties, set down his Tecate beer and ambled toward the dance floor. Mona, catching sight of him, leaned in toward Heather.

"Oh my, I think we have a lumberjack headed our way," she shouted over the throbbing music, nodding at the plaid-shirted man who was now smiling and dancing nearby.

As the song ended and another 1970s disco classic began, the infectious rhythm kept everyone on the floor. By the end of two more songs, Plaid Shirt and Heather had drifted apart from the others, each showcasing their dance moves to the other.

"I need to catch my breath," Heather finally shouted to the man towering over her. In her flats, she stood a modest five-foot-three. He was imposing, rugged, and stood a foot taller.

"My name is Dutch. Thanks for the dances." His voice was warm and friendly.

Heather told him her name and added that everyone called her Red. Then she made her way back to her friends, her cheeks flushed with exertion and exhilaration. She thought the name Dutch suited him—his heritage was surely Northern European.

Mona and Laurie were still on the dance floor, caught in the music's spell, but Kim was returning from the bar with a tray of tequila shots.

The birthday celebration surged on with more dancing, more shots, and cascades of laughter. Dutch and his friends eventually joined them on the dance floor, the night swirling into a blur of joyous revelry and newfound connections. By midnight, the eight had pulled a couple of tables together, expanding the festivity.

Conversation was limited by the volume of the music, but the DJ took a couple of breaks throughout the evening, giving the new friends a chance to talk. Dutch and Heather, both smokers, wandered out to the walkway a couple of times to satisfy their addiction. They chatted about San Amaro and the Baja in general.

Heather learned Dutch and his buddies were from Denver, where he was a logistics manager for the state government. The men were all motorcycle enthusiasts returning home from a trip to Cabo San Lucas on their dual-sport bikes. This was the four men's last night in Mexico.

As they stood talking and smoking, neither noticed the man in a pickup truck parked on the Malecon. When Dutch held the door for Heather and they disappeared back inside, the driver tossed binoculars onto the passenger seat with such force that the eye cushion on one of the lenses popped off and landed on the floor. He angrily grabbed a beer from the six-pack he'd bought for his stakeout, opened it, and took a long pull.

Damn her. The alcohol ignited a blaze of distrust and jealousy that consumed his mind. His imagination ran wild, each thought more sinister than the last as he pictured what might be happening inside the throbbing walls of the Cha-Cha Club. He clenched his fists, fury surging through his veins.

He lingered in the shadows, eyes locked on the club's front door, waiting for the perfect moment to strike.

Chapter Two – Present Day

Abe Walker, a lanky Texan, strode into the sales office of Cortez Oasis, the sandy parking lot crunching under his boots. He'd noticed the sign three days ago when he drove into San Amaro, and curiosity had tugged at his mind ever since. The building was a squat, unassuming structure nestled across the highway from the main entrance to the Oasis, the name the locals used to refer to the sprawling gated community.

San Amaro, a fishing village of slightly over 17,000, hugged the Sea of Cortez, on the east side of the Baja peninsula. Over the past three decades, it had become a retirement destination for Canadians, Americans, and Europeans. Unlike Cabo, Puerto Vallarta it remained mostly ungentrified. The Oasis and a few, much smaller communities surrounding San Amaro were home to the growing expat community, most of them retirees.

Inside the sales office, Walker was greeted by a short, stocky man dressed in shorts, a Hawaiian shirt, and deck shoes without socks.

"Hi! I'm Willie Platz. Are you here to buy, rent, or look at building lots?" He extended his hand with a welcoming smile. The sales office focused on selling vacant lots and existing homes not listed by one of the other two realtors in town. Few people were shopping for vacant lots.

Abe grasped the extended hand firmly, offering a brief nod. “I’m interested in homes for sale.”

As Platz and Walker discussed available properties and Abe’s preferences, Abe’s eyes roamed the office. It was a modest 400-square-foot space with a coffee station, a bathroom, and three metal office desks with dated wood-patterned Arborite tops. Cream-painted walls were adorned with maps of the Cortez Oasis communities and listings of houses and lots for sale.

Despite having researched extensively before arriving, Abe Walker was still taken aback by the sheer size of the 35,000-acre community depicted on the maps. Of the thousands of lots shown on the maps, only a fraction showed the red dot of ownership. The 2008 housing crash put a hard stop to the Oasis’s building boom. Holiday homes in Mexico were only recently becoming popular and financially viable again.

The sun’s scorching rays warned of a blistering day ahead as the two men climbed into one of three aging Ford Escapes parked outside, each bearing the Oasis logo. The cloth seats were worn, but the vehicle was clean and the air conditioner mercifully efficient. They had four houses to view, scattered across the fifty-four square miles of the community.

Highway Five—the main north-south artery on Baja’s eastern side—split the Oasis in two: the mountain side to the west, and the sea side bordering the Sea of Cortez to the east. All four houses Abe wanted to see were on the mountain side. The first, nestled in a densely populated area near the main swimming pool complex and close to the highway, was the smallest on Abe’s list. One look and he knew it wasn’t what he wanted; he wanted more space and solitude.

As was his custom with new clients, Willie stopped at the pools to showcase the amenities. The beauty of the facilities struck Abe. A brightly colored tiled mural graced one wall of the building housing the showers and bathrooms. The three pools—a general swimming pool, an activity pool, and a giant hot tub—were crystal clear, surrounded by inviting lounge chairs, some shaded by arching sailcloth and others basking in the full sun.

A water aerobics class was underway in the activity pool, with a couple of dozen people splashing to the leader's rhythm and the piped-in music. Fifteen or twenty others lounged beside the swimming pool or swam laps. The hot tub, for the moment, lay dormant. Willie, ever the salesman, emphasized that no other community near San Amaro could match these exclusive facilities.

After a long drive toward the mountains, the second house left Abe disheartened. The size and floor plan were ideal, but its remote location and complete dependence on solar power made it impractical. Without electricity or significantly more solar panels and batteries, the house couldn't generate enough power to run air conditioning during Baja's hot summer nights—a necessity for full-time living. Willie admitted that the house wouldn't meet Abe's needs without the costly addition of more solar components.

The final two homes were located at the northern end of the Oasis. Upon viewing them, Abe finally felt a glimmer of hope. He liked both. Standing in the yard of the last house, Abe noted its fully fenced yard—perfect for his eighty-pound Rottweiler, Benny. The house boasted three spacious bedrooms, kitchen and dining area in an open-plan style, and three bathrooms. A sunken spot in the brick patio, however, caught his discerning eye.

“What do you suppose is causing the dip there?” Abe’s curiosity was piqued.

“I couldn’t say. But I can recommend a builder who can inspect the place and give you a full rundown. San Amaro doesn’t have designated home inspectors. As with so many things here, you’ll find people wear multiple hats. And things are much more casual here than in the States or even in cities like Guadalajara and Mexico City.”

Abe decided to have the last two houses inspected. Either could meet his needs, and they were similarly priced. The fenced yard, however, might tip the scales. As Willie drove them back to the sales office, Abe called José Amaya, the builder, and arranged for an inspection of both properties the following day.

Shortly after ten the next morning, Walker and Platz met the builder at the sales office, and he followed them to the first house. Like all the roads on the Oasis, the street was compacted sand that had been watered down and graded. The moisture had long since evaporated, and dust clouds billowed behind both vehicles.

The first house was currently rented to a Mexican family visiting from Mexicali for the week. Willie had explained that San Amaro, though only two hours away, was a popular getaway for Mexicali residents. Nestled against the Sea of Cortez, the tiny town of San Amaro provided water sports, off-road adventures, and a welcome escape from the million-plus people living in Mexicali. The renting family was heading to the beach when Abe, Willie, and the builder arrived.

The inspection revealed a few minor issues inside the house that needed attention, but nothing serious enough to deter Abe from keeping it on his list. As they caravaned to the second house, Abe queried Willie about the house-buying process in Mexico as an American.

He'd heard about something called a *fideicomiso* but wasn't sure what it was, how one was obtained, or what it would cost. Willie explained that it was a legal trust through a Mexican bank—the only way foreigners could hold title to property within the restricted zones in Mexico.

The second house, which had sat vacant for more than fifteen years, took longer to inspect. As with any structure left to the elements, there were numerous repairs needed, but the interior was clean and tidy. After finishing the interior inspection, Amaya turned his attention to the sunken area in the brick patio.

He examined it closely but finally said he'd need to remove the bricks to determine the cause. Willie would have to contact the homeowner for permission to dismantle the patio.

Chapter Three – Present Day

Jeremy Filbert was a dutiful son. For years he made the trek from his home in Sacramento to visit his mom in the tiny town of Crows Landing, where he'd grown up.

The drive took more than three hours round-trip, but today would be the last time he'd make the familiar journey. His mom's dementia had worsened significantly, and she rarely recognized him anymore. Finding a care worker in Crows Landing—population three hundred—was impossible, and finding one willing to travel there was becoming equally so. Work in Sacramento and Stockton was plentiful.

Jeremy and his sister, Jen, had discussed moving their mom to Sacramento. They'd put Rosemary's name on the waiting list for Raulston Manor, a highly regarded residential memory care facility for individuals with Alzheimer's and other types of dementia. A room had just become available.

When Jeremy arrived, his mom recognized him and even called him by his name. It seemed like today was a good day for his mom. However, within minutes, it became clear that she thought he was her long-deceased husband, not her son—both named Jeremy. Still, she was more lucid than she had been in weeks, which, as it turned out, was a stroke of luck.

Shortly after Jeremy arrived, the phone rang. He picked up the old landline receiver—the same one he'd used as a child—and answered as he'd been taught those many years before.

"Filbert residence."

"Hi, is Rosemary Filbert there?" asked the caller.

After asking who was calling and why, Jeremy explained his mother's condition and that he was now handling her affairs. The caller, Willie Platz of San Amaro, Baja, Mexico, described the issue with his mother's property there and asked about removing the patio to investigate the problem.

"Are you sure you've got the right property?" Jeremy asked. "It's been close to twenty years since I've been there, but I don't remember any brick patio. I thought the yard was mostly sand with a couple of planters along the fence."

Since Rosemary could sometimes recall past events more clearly than recent ones, Jeremy asked Willie to hold while he checked with her. She adamantly confirmed that there had never been a brick patio in the yard. Willie double-checked the address with Jeremy and informed him that there were bricks there now.

Several months earlier, Jeremy and Jen decided it was time to sell the property in Mexico to help cover the costs of their mother's care. Jen handled arranging for someone to clean and declutter the home—another strain on their already limited funds. So, in the excitement of hearing someone was possibly interested in buying it, the mystery of the patio's existence was of little importance, and permission was granted for the builder to investigate the cause of the sinkage.

After getting the go-ahead, the wheels were put in motion to have José Amaya remove the brickwork.

José and a small crew arrived at the property shortly after eight the next morning, the workers riding in the box of the twenty-five-year-old pickup truck.

Fortunately, the bricks had not been cemented in place. They had been laid on the sand, with more sand used to fill the cracks between them. The young men removed the bricks, row by row, stacking them against the wall of the garage.

They were shocked at what lay beneath the sagging patio.

Chapter Four - Present Day

The small station house of the San Amaro branch of the Baja State Police housed nineteen officers, a two-cell jail, and a small, inadequately equipped forensics lab. Shortly before lunch, the desk sergeant transferred a call to Detective Sergeant Julia Garcia's desk phone, stating simply that the caller only spoke English. Julia was the only fully bilingual officer in the station.

Standing a statuesque five-foot-nine, Julia commanded attention the moment she entered a room. Her black hair, worn in a bun at the nape of her neck, framed a face defined by both strength and warmth. Her brown eyes, sharp and vigilant, carried an unexpected softness—a quiet kindness. Her firm voice, though never harsh, carried the weight of experience beyond her thirty-some years.

She listened closely to the caller, making notes, asking clarifying questions, and verifying the man's location. When she hung up, she motioned to her partner, Detective Sergeant Hernandez.

"We've got a case. It's out at the Oasis. I'll grab La Chica and meet you out in the lot." She made one other quick call before leaving the building.

La Chica was Julia's battered and aging brown Honda Civic. As a detective, she had the option to use her personal car or a squad vehicle. She preferred her own car. Police cars, in her experience, made people nervous. She liked to begin from a neutral position. There'd be time for stronger tactics later, if needed.

The officers of the San Amaro State Police were underpaid and underfunded. San Amaro, having recently gained status as its own municipality, was no longer governed by Mexicali. This was both good and bad for the local police. Having the tax dollars from San Amaro residents stay in their town meant the local police might get a small raise or have money for better equipment. However, it also meant they could no longer rely on services from Mexicali, like advanced forensics. The small force was scrambling to fill the gaps and often had to get creative.

During the drive, Julia updated Ricardo. Human remains had been found in an old cistern on an abandoned property at the northern edge of the Oasis community. Julia's last-minute call had been to Andrés Alvarez, a nurse trained in forensics who worked with Dr. Serrano, their GP-turned-coroner.

Andrés had completed two accredited courses in crime-scene forensics offered by the US State Department at a university in Mexicali. The training was part of a bilateral effort to reduce cartel violence by ensuring forensic evidence was properly collected and handled. Conviction rates had improved on both sides of the border as a result. Andrés assured Julia he and Dr. Serrano would meet them at the appropriate security gate into the Oasis.

While they waited for the medical duo to join them, Julia finished her recap of the call. The previous day, Willie Platz, a real estate agent for the Oasis, had shown the property to a prospective buyer named Abe Walker.

Walker, concerned about a sunken area in the brick patio, arranged to have some of the bricks removed to determine the cause. That morning, the contractor discovered a partially collapsed water cistern under the patio. Inside it were human remains.

Contrary to common assumption, the desert upon which the Oasis was built, far from being a vast and vacant expanse of sand, was alive with vegetation and wildlife. Many types of cacti, creosote bushes, thousands of ocotillos, and trees—mesquite, elephant, and the occasional paloverde—were scattered around Oasis and the property where the remains had been discovered.

Once the police and medical team arrived at the Filbert house, they used José's ladder, carefully lowering it down into the cistern. José had already connected a work light to his truck battery to illuminate the underground tank. Ricardo, slightly senior to Julia, was the first to enter the tank.

The cistern was a concrete cube of about nine or ten feet per side. The hinges of the hatch's drop-down door had long since rusted through. The door, about three feet square, now lay on the floor of the tank. A few feet away was a skeleton.

A piece of plywood covered the cistern entry hole. Over the years, rain and heat had rotted the board, causing the ground above it to sink. That was the depression Abe Walker had noticed.

The skeleton lay in a heap near the back corner. After inspecting the bones, Dr. Serrano pronounced the body was that of a woman. An indentation at the base of her skull suggested foul play. When Julia pushed him to give an estimate of the time of death, he hesitated but finally said that, based on the degree of weathering of the bones, it could be from ten to twenty years ago. A full examination at the hospital would hopefully provide more details.

As Dr. Serrano discussed his findings, Andrés photographed everything *in situ.* He then proceeded to collect evidence.

There wasn't much to collect. The cistern, built to hold water, was, apart from the missing door, intact and made of concrete. Apart from bones, some hair, and bits of clothing, the tank now contained only sand and debris from the collapsed hatch.

Andrés sealed the samples in evidence bags. As he moved back toward the ladder with his collection, a glint caught his eye. He used his phone flashlight to investigate further and discovered a short piece of fine gold chain under a dusting of sand. This also went into an evidence bag. All the evidence was then locked in a case bolted to the floor in the trunk of *La Chica*.

While the forensic work was underway, Ricardo questioned José Amaya, and Julia interviewed the realtor and his buyer. Amaya told Ricardo that a cistern of this type would have had a small pump house beside it to move water into the home's plumbing system. The absence of such a structure meant the house didn't currently have operational plumbing. Based on the sun-fading on the patio bricks, he estimated the patio was likely at least ten years old.

Julia took statements from Willie and Abe and informed them they would likely be contacted again as the investigation progressed. Willie provided Julia with the property owner's contact information, explaining that Mrs. Rosemary Filbert had abandoned the home nearly sixteen years ago, after her husband's death.

Julia and Ricardo took photos of the property and surrounding area before heading back to the station with the forensic evidence. Julia noted four other houses within a half-mile radius of the site and suggested they start interviewing neighbors after dropping off the forensics at the lab.

The Cortez Oasis had been established in the late 1980s but didn't begin to flourish until the early 2000s. Like much of North America, it boomed during the mid-2000s. But when the 2008 housing crash hit, Baja felt the impact even harder.

Many of the homes in San Amaro had been built as vacation properties by non-Mexican owners, and in the post-2008 world, few people were building second homes—especially not in Baja.

While the US and Canada slowly recovered from the economic turmoil, expat-driven construction in Mexico continued to decline. Housing developments in Baja were left with hundreds of vacant lots. Many areas of the Oasis looked like a thousand-piece jigsaw puzzle missing nine hundred of its pieces.

As the car hummed along the road, Ricardo broke the silence. "Since neither of us has ever worked on a cold case, maybe we should speak with Detective Inspector Martinez. He might have some insights on how to move forward."

"Someone killed that person. How will we ever figure out who?"

Chapter Five – Fifteen Years Ago

Malcolm Davenport crushed his third can of Tecate Red since parking on the street across from the Cha-Cha Club and made a decision. Watching the entrance with binoculars hadn't produced another glimpse of his girlfriend and the tall, blond dude in the plaid shirt.

He needed to see inside the club to get a better sense of what was going on. He was convinced that Heather—Red, as he called her—was fooling around with that guy, whoever he was, but he needed proof.

He wove unsteadily up the stairs to the walkway to the club's entrance. The thrum of the dance music hit him like a punch to the gut; it was deafening. Even in his drunken haze, Malcolm recognized the building's design—it had been an icehouse.

As a former commercial fisherman, he immediately noticed the trapdoor through the metal gridwork of the raised walkway. Before the building became a nightclub, San Amaro fishermen would pull their boats into the slip below to receive a dump of ice into their fish holds.

The club was packed. It took Malcolm a minute to scan the room before his eyes landed on Heather and her friends. He zeroed in on the table of four men and four women, its surface cluttered with empty shot glasses and beer cans.

His anger surged. She was a lying bitch. So much for a birthday dinner and dancing with "just three girlfriends." The eight people around that table seemed pretty chummy.

He'd deal with her later. No point making a scene with so many people around.

Back in his truck, another beer in hand, Malcolm decided he'd wait it out. The club would close in less than an hour, then Heather would have to come out. They'd talk then.

He was sure Red was cheating. Not just flirting—cheating. Laughing, touching, leaning in close. He could see it all in his mind. She'd probably already kissed that guy. Probably more. She was always like that, slutty. Redheads. What was he even doing with her anymore?

At one-thirty, the lights in the club flicked on and off—last call. Dutch, Heather, and the rest of the group downed the last of their drinks and began saying their goodbyes.

"What a great ending to a wonderful trip." Dutch and his buddies stood to leave the club. "I really enjoyed meeting you, Red. Thanks for the dances. If you ever find yourself in Denver, look me up." He handed her a business card with his home phone number scribbled on the back.

"I had fun too, Dutch. Have a safe trip home."

When he leaned over to hug her, Heather kissed his cheek and whispered something in his ear. He smiled and gave her a wink before he and his friends left.

Malcolm watched the four men leave the club together and head toward a hotel down the street. He waited a couple more minutes, expecting to see Heather and her friends emerge. Growing impatient, he left his truck and again climbed the stairs to the bar. Without the thrum of music, the place felt strangely hollow. Most of the patrons had already left. Heather and her friends were headed toward the exit as Malcolm stumbled through the door.

Heather said something to her friends before walking to where Malcolm stood, just inside the doors. The other women headed out and called a final goodbye to Heather, giving Malcolm a nod of acknowledgment as they passed him.

"This is a surprise, Malc," she said, smiling. "I didn't expect a ride home. I thought you and your buddies would still be playing poker." She was happy. It had been a fun night, but those happy feelings didn't last long.

"Who the hell was that tall blond guy you were cozied up to all night?"

"What? Were you spying on me? You're drunk." Her voice was thick with disgust. But she knew from experience that Malcolm wouldn't let it drop. "He was just some guy I danced with. He and his buddies are passing through. We had a couple drinks with them. It was nothing. So why *are* you even here? You knew Mona was going to drive me home."

"I wasn't spying," Malcolm lied. "I just wanted to drive you home myself. I sent the poker gang home early so I could come get you. Come on. Let's go."

"I think I need the little girl's room first. I'll be right back." Heather turned away and headed toward the back of the club.

Malcolm loitered near the bar, watching the bartender wrap up for the night while the last few remaining partiers stumbled out. He soon grew restless and wandered to the restrooms. After banging on the door to the ladies' room and getting no response, he pushed it open. Heather was the sole occupant of the room, standing by the sink, washing her hands.

"Taking your time, aren't you? Let's go. Now!"

"Don't yell at me, Malcolm. I'm almost done."

The fluorescent lights buzzed overhead. The floor was sticky. The whole place reeked of bleach, tequila, and sweat—like a place that had seen too many bad decisions.

She was trying to provoke him; he knew it. They often fought about how long it took her to get ready, how she made them late. Alcohol-fueled delusions filled him with rage. He grabbed her arm, intending to drag her out to the truck if he had to. He wasn't putting up with her games. Not tonight.

But Heather saw it coming. As he grabbed her, she jerked back, unbalancing them both. She slipped, fell backward, and struck her head on the edge of the counter before collapsing to the floor. The crack of her head hitting the counter made Malcolm's stomach lurch. For a second, everything went still—his rage gone, his hands suddenly useless.

Then Malcolm dropped to her side in panic. "Oh my God! Are you okay? What the hell were you doing? I wasn't going to hurt you." He hovered over her. She blinked up at him, dazed, and tried unsuccessfully to sit up. Malcolm helped her, inspecting her head.

"It looks okay—just a little broken skin at your hairline. It's bleeding a bit." He grabbed some paper towels. "Here, this'll take care of it. Do you feel alright to stand?"

He was helping her to her feet when the bathroom door opened. A janitor pushed a rolling mop bucket into the room. The initial shock of finding people in the bathroom registered on her face, then was quickly replaced by indignation.

Though her angry tirade was entirely in Spanish, it was clear she thought the couple was using the room for a sexual encounter. Looking at the filthy floor, they both shuddered at the thought. Rather than try to explain in their broken Spanish, they simply left.

Heather leaned heavily on Malcolm for support as they walked to the truck. He muttered they'd likely laugh about it tomorrow.

He was wrong.

Chapter Six – Present Day

Julia transferred custody of the forensics collected from the cistern to the police forensics expert, Vicente Pessoa. On paper, he was the station's forensics expert—though Julia often considered the term *expert* a bit generous.

Compared to previous lab techs, Vicente was a clear improvement. But compared to a graduate of a formal forensic science program, he still had some distance to go.

He'd completed nearly two years of a four-year degree and had handled evidence competently in several important cases. Julia had no qualms about entrusting him with the evidence collected at the scene.

Vicente had been with the San Amaro police for nearly two years, having left university in his second year of a four-year forensic science degree. His grandfather, diagnosed with terminal stomach cancer at the time, needed live-in assistance. Vicente's dad had promised his son he could return to his studies when the grandfather passed.

Vicente's family was from Oaxaca, over three thousand miles away. His grandfather, a metallurgical engineer, had moved to San Amaro before Vicente was born to work in the gold mine north of town. When his grandfather was diagnosed, Vicente was the family member most able to take a hiatus from his life to stay with his dying abuelo.

Julia knew that when the old man died, Vicente would be leaving them and returning to university in Guadalajara. He was the best forensics technician the station had had. He would be sorely missed. And, given that she'd just learned that his grandfather had recently gone into hospice care, she suspected it would be soon.

The cistern had yielded very little: a rusty ladder, scraps of fabric, some hair, and a small gold stud with a fine gold chain dangling from it. As Vicente logged the items into evidence, Julia inspected the fabric through its sealed bag. Though the cloth was caked with sand and grime, a faint shimmering beneath the dirt caught her eye.

"Vicente, when you analyze the fabric, please clean one of the larger bits up so I can see the pattern on the material. I think the woman might have been dressed up, maybe for a special occasion. Perhaps it can provide a lead."

"Will do," he replied easily. "Is it a high priority?"

"What else are you working on?"

Vicente explained his workload and other cases that had evidence to be analyzed. Together, they prioritized a couple of activities ahead of hers. Their skeleton had been dead a long time; a couple more days wouldn't make much difference. She would have his analysis and the cleaned material soon enough.

Julia walked up the hall to speak with Detective Inspector Martinez, her direct supervisor and the person who had encouraged and mentored Julia's rise to detective sergeant. Martinez was an intelligent, soft-spoken man in his fifties. His brown hair, now graying at the temples, and his hazel eyes often confused local expats into thinking he was American…until he tried to speak English.

Julia requested two constables to help gather background information on their case. Martinez agreed. She assigned Constable

Luis Flores the job of digging through all unsolved missing-person cases from the past twenty years.

For the second assignment, Julia deliberately chose Constable Ana Maria Verde—one of the few female officers on the force, she was rarely assigned work in the field. Usually she was stuck doing desk tasks like filing or records searches. But Julia was giving Ana Maria a more substantial role, though still mostly file searches.

Today, she was to go to the homeowner's association offices at the Oasis and uncover the names of property owners within a one-kilometer radius of the location of the remains.

The Oasis used a convoluted and elaborate numbering scheme for each lot. Without the detailed plat map—which the HOA guarded like gold—it was nearly impossible to find a given property within the labyrinthine road structure.

Residents either provided directions such as "Go straight from the third gate for a half mile, then turn left at the cactus that looks like a…" or met people at the gate and led them to their homes. A few of the technology-savvy residents sent people a GPS pin to direct them.

With those assignments made, Julia searched for Ricardo, finally finding him drawing on a whiteboard in the upstairs conference room. He explained the room was available to them as a war room for their investigation. After a moment, she realized he'd neatly drawn out the property where the body was found.

"Wow, Ricky, that's great." And she meant it. He was famous for illegible writing, so the tidy drawing was a surprise.

Julia used his nickname from their days at the police academy. Their fellow cadets dubbed them Lucy and Ricky, partly because Ricardo closely resembled Desi Arnaz, but mostly because they were always bickering and goading each other. All in fun.

They had both been hired by the San Amaro Police upon graduation and continued with the fun, a legacy of their shared past.

Only this time, Ricardo didn't respond in kind. He looked at her with a solemn mask but said nothing.

Julia knew why, but was still disheartened by his lack of response. Nonetheless, she told him about their two constables and her assignments to them in the same light tone.

They got down to the business of figuring out how they might proceed to solve this seemingly ancient murder.

Someone, somewhere, knew what had happened to that woman.

Chapter Seven – Fifteen Years Ago

During the twenty-five-minute drive from the club to their home, Malcolm's benevolent mood slowly dissolved, uncovering the simmering anger and jealousy lurking beneath the surface. On the first part of the drive, he peppered Heather with questions about the blond man he'd seen her with. By the time they neared their house, his abuse had turned malignant.

Heather leaned forward in her seat, cradling her head in her hands as if trying to hold together the fractured pieces of her skull. The excruciating pain was exacerbated by too much tequila and his vicious tirade. She gritted her teeth to defend herself against both.

Slut. Whore. Bitch.

His words were sharp, but only a few cut through the relentless throbbing in her head. Her silence was gasoline to his fury until he smacked her hard in the face.

Her world went black.

Malcolm didn't immediately realize what he'd done. Heather was still slumped forward, but no longer held her head. She sagged limply against the seatbelt. When he yanked the truck door open to make her get out, her head flopped back, revealing a gaping, bloody mouth and lifeless eyes staring into eternity.

It was the early hours of the morning, and under the new moon, the world was cloaked in shadows. Panic hit first, then fear, sharp and overwhelming. His alcohol-blurred mind struggling to process the scene in front of him.

He paced in frantic circles around the truck, trying to figure out what to do. There were no houses near his, so he wasn't worried about prying eyes. Then he remembered: the owner of the closest house had recently died, leaving his home abandoned.

A plan began to form.

On the west side of the Oasis—the mountain side—each property was equipped with a cistern for water and a septic tank for wastewater, as there was no public sewer or water supply. Both were typically buried underground, made of reinforced concrete with manholes or a trapdoor to provide access for filling or emptying.

Driving without headlights, Malcolm crept toward the deserted property. Under the dim light of a flashlight, he located the cistern hatch. After several attempts, he managed to unlatch its heavy lid. Inside, the tank was mostly dry, with just a few inches of water remaining at the bottom.

A small ladder, once used for maintenance, leaned against a crumbling wall of what had once been the pump house. He dropped it into place.

He'd planned to carry Heather's limp corpse down the ladder, but the hatch wasn't wide enough to accommodate his and Heather's bodies. Instead, he dumped her remains into the cavernous reservoir with a grunt. Breathless and shaking, he climbed down and dragged her body as far from the opening as possible.

His heart slammed against his ribcage hard enough that he thought his chest would explode. Halfway back to the truck, he stopped, turned around, and returned to throw the ladder into the tank too. He slammed the hatch shut and drove off, taking the same slow, silent route back.

Once home, he found a nearly full bottle of whiskey and drank himself into oblivion.

Anything to avoid thinking about what he'd just done.

Chapter Eight – Present Day

When Julia called the owner of the property where the remains had been found, she spoke with the son, Jeremy, and quickly learned of his mother's condition.

Julia questioned him about the cistern, the property, and whether the house had ever been a rental. It soon became clear that his knowledge of San Amaro and his parents' property there was too limited to be useful. The only helpful detail he provided was that the house had been vacant for the past sixteen years.

Jeremy was stunned to learn that the skeleton—likely a murdered woman—had been discovered on the property. He promised he'd try talking with his mom about it in her more lucid moments, but he warned that those moments were rare. Regardless, he doubted she'd know anything useful.

Later, Julia and Ricardo sat in their makeshift war room. While they waited for the coroner's report, any findings from Ana Maria's research into nearby property owners, updates from Luis's review of missing person cases, or Vicente's forensic analysis, they researched the Filbert family members.

The body had been found on their property, after all. Perhaps they had left San Amaro to escape a crime. Ricardo got off the phone. "The *Instituto Nacional de Migración* has no record of any of the Filberts being issued a visa in the past fifteen years."

"Unfortunately, that's not conclusive. We both know that many people cross the border from the States and never get a visa."

"Did you find anything from your research?"

Julia flipped back in her notebook before answering. "Jeremy Filbert senior died more than sixteen years ago. Their kids are both in their fifties. Their mom is in her mid-seventies and has been suffering from dementia for more than eight years. It's not much yet, but I'll keep digging."

So far, they knew only that the remains were female. And now, thanks to Jeremy, they knew the body had likely been deposited in the cistern sometime within the last sixteen years. Judging from the weathered condition of the bones, Julia and Ricardo estimated that the death had occurred more than ten years ago. Until the coroner gave them something more precise, they decided to focus on a ten-to-fifteen-year timeframe.

Ricardo, finishing his fourth coffee of the morning, stood and stretched. "I can't sit here any longer. Let's start talking to people who live nearby. We might learn more about the Filberts. We can refine our canvass once Ana Maria gets back to us with her findings."

On the drive to the Oasis, they stopped at HOA office where they found Ana Maria poring over a stack of files in a small office separate from the public area. She provided them with the names and property numbers of the two nearby owners she'd found so far who'd lived there within their time of death window. It was enough to get them started.

Because the Oasis was so large and only sparsely occupied, there were often considerable distances between homes. Such was the case with the Filbert house. The nearest neighbor lived on the next street, several hundred yards away. According to Ana Maria's notes, the residents were Tom and Angie Hovart.

"Mrs. Hovart?" Julia asked, correctly assuming the woman didn't speak enough Spanish to be conversant. The attractive woman in her sixties, dressed in a tank top, shorts, and sandals. she confirmed her identity. Julia introduced herself and Ricardo and explained the reason for their visit.

"A dead body!" Angie exclaimed. After a moment to gather herself, she invited them in.

Once seated—and Julia and Ricardo had politely declined the offer of lemonade—Julia provided a few more details, saying only that the deceased was female and had been in the cistern for the past ten to fifteen years.

"You mean that there's been a dead woman lying in a water tank just over there all these years?" Angie shuddered. "Oh, my Lord."

The woman crossed herself with her last words. Catholic, Julia noted.

"How long have you and your husband lived here, Mrs. Hovart?" Julia began her questions.

"We've lived in San Amaro for almost eighteen years. We met the Filberts a couple of times, but didn't know them well."

"Did you socialize at all with the Filberts when they were still coming here?"

Angie shook her.

"You have a good view of their house. Did you notice any activity there in the last fifteen years? Contractors, perhaps?"

Angie shook her head again. "Not that I recall."

"Do you know of anyone who was living in the area during that time who's since moved away?"

"Oh yes, someone lived just north of here who moved out…maybe seven or eight years ago?" I didn't know him, though. I think a younger couple is living there now, but I don't know them either. I'm so busy with my church, I don't socialize much…" Angie's voice faded out.

Julia had the sense she was about to add, *especially not with people outside the congregation*.

"Might your husband be more familiar with your neighbors?" Julia hoped to get something useful from this visit.

"Possibly. He's at water volleyball—goes every day. You could try phoning him after one-thirty." She gave Julia his cell number.

"We'd like to keep this off Facebook and out of the gossip loop for a few days, if possible," Julia said. "Would you mind keeping it to yourself for now?"

"I'm not on Facebook." Angie waved her hand. "And, as I said, I don't socialize much."

Julia thanked the woman, and she and Ricardo returned to the car. As they buckled in, Julia turned to her partner. "Maybe the next couple will have something more useful. I'm already getting frustrated with the lack of progress on this case.

"I get it. But we *are* making progress. It's just slow. We have neighbors here to interview, and we'll have more information soon. I can feel it."

Julia gave him credit for his optimism. Something was bound to turn up soon.

Chapter Nine – Present Day

Several years ago, Julia, still a young sergeant handling menial tasks, had been assigned as the police liaison on a missing person case involving an English-speaking resident of San Amaro who had vanished during a mountain hike with friends. That woman was Stella Monroe.

Shortly after escaping an elaborate murder plot and being held captive by a human trafficker for nearly two weeks, Stella had inherited several million dollars. She vowed to use it to help trafficked women. Her long-time friend, Pippa, had moved to San Amaro around the same time and was eager to be involved. Julia had agreed to help them in any way she could.

Earlier in the week, Stella, a long-time resident of San Amaro, had left a phone message to invite Julia to dinner to talk with her about the nonprofit she was starting with her inheritance. When Julia returned the call, they made the date for that night.

"That would be lovely, Julia. I'll see if Pippa can join us. She's an important part of this venture."

The women agreed to meet at six at La Casita. Julia was thrilled with the choice of venue—it was one of her favorite restaurants. Though well-known and much-loved by the locals, La Casita remained a hidden gem few expats had discovered. Leaving work, she figured she would have enough time to grab a shower before meeting up with Pippa and Stella at the restaurant.

It took Stella a moment to recognize Julia when she entered La Casita. Julia's lustrous black hair, usually worn in a tight bun, hung in loose waves over the shoulders of a cream-colored sweater-dress that accentuated her natural curves. It was the first time she'd seen the woman with her hair down and dressed casually—the softer side of the off-duty police officer.

The intoxicating aromas from the surrounding tables reminded Julia why she loved this place. She was glad she'd missed lunch. The three ordered their meals, each choosing a different fish dish, and chatted about the restaurant and other light topics. As the plates were cleared away and the last drops of wine were poured, Stella leaned in, ready to turn the conversation to the purpose of the evening.

"Julia, thank you for being willing to chat with us about the charity I want to start. I have to be honest, in the last few weeks, I've been reading everything I can find about human trafficking, and I guess I didn't have any idea what all it entailed. I'm not even sure what we," Stella motioned to herself and Pippa, "can do about it or what San Amaro needs in that regard. Do you have any insight, as a police officer, which might help us narrow down such a huge issue into a more focused area where we could make a difference?"

"It's an issue about which I don't feel very educated, actually," Julia said. "Why don't you tell me what your thoughts are, and maybe that will help me to be of more value to you."

Stella and Pippa shared their initial research on human trafficking in Baja and beyond. Julia listened intently, impressed by the statistics, stories, and insights they'd uncovered. When they finished, Julia felt like she'd just taken a university course.

"Wow! You've done your homework." Julia's head was swimming. "I'm embarrassed by how little I knew about this before tonight. I have degrees in psychology and criminology, but most of what you've just told me is news. I suspect it's the same for many of my peers in law enforcement here in San Amaro."

Julia continued. "There are three separate police forces here. First, there's the Federales, recently renamed the Guardia Nacional. They're responsible for tackling organized crime and cartel activity. Then there's the State Police, like me. We work on major crimes like kidnapping, drug trafficking, murder, and traffic issues on the highways. Finally, there's the Municipal Police. They patrol neighborhoods and downtown and cover minor crimes like small thefts, public disorder, that kind of thing."

Pippa sipped the remaining wine in her glass. "Thank you for explaining that. I've always wondered who did what."

"Developing a training program for officers could raise awareness of what to look for and how to approach suspected trafficking cases. And, because children are so often targets, an awareness campaign for the schools here might help protect them. Those seem like logical first steps that could lead you to discover what other needs exist here in San Amaro."

Stella and Pippa exchanged glances, both nodding. "That sounds like a brilliant way to start," Pippa said. "This makes so much sense."

For the next half-hour, the three discussed how two American women with limited Spanish skills could navigate a project of this scale in Baja. Julia provided practical advice, and by the time they left the restaurant, Stella and Pippa felt more confident, ready to take the next steps.

Chapter Ten – Fifteen Years Ago

The day after he'd disposed of her body, Malcolm had awoken with a hangover like none before. Unable to keep even water down, he'd returned to bed, sleeping fitfully for several more hours. On the bedside table was a spiral-bound notebook, his daily journal for tracking the day's weather, noting wind speed, temperatures, rain—what little of it there was—and any major events that might have occurred. That day, during one of his waking moments, he picked it up.

His fragmented dreams had been filled with ghouls, dark caverns, and death, and he awoke in a miasma of fear. Lying in his sweat-soaked, stale-smelling bed, he decided he needed to get his story straight. Finding a clean page in his journal, he began to create his fiction.

Saturday, Oct 9, 2010 Red (Heather) and I got home late last night after she'd been out with her girlfriends. I picked her up from the Cha-Cha Club at closing time. On the drive home, she told me she was going to leave me today. I have never been that serious about her, so it isn't a big deal to me. Today, she packed up her clothes and loaded them in her car and left. I ain't seen her since.

He left a gap of a few lines in his journal, then continued.

I called her a few days later to make sure she was okay, but the phone must a been turned off or something.

A few weeks later, she called me from a different number to say she was settled in a new place and was working as a bartender. She never said where she was, but it sounded like she was at a party or working at the bar with lots of loud people.

Malcolm stopped and reread what he'd written so far. It sounded plausible. It was a start. He could add more as needed. He tried to imagine how he'd feel in that situation. If he wasn't supposed to have been that into her, he likely wouldn't be angry or upset. He might even be glad to be free of her, or at least more available to do things with his buddies.

He reread his story one more time and realized with a jolt that he had to do something with her car and clothes immediately. But what?

He dragged himself out of bed and into a hot shower. It helped him wake up, but more importantly, it allowed him to think more clearly. Dressed and with a piece of toast in his belly, he started to feel almost human. He loaded everything of Heather's he could find into suitcases and a couple of boxes and packed up her car.

He'd removed the license plates before he left San Amaro and tossed them into a dumpster behind a gas station where he'd filled up on his way over the mountains to the coastal border town, Tijuana, of more than two million residents. He drove the car into a poor neighborhood in Tijuana and left it unlocked with the keys in the ignition. It would not remain there long, he was sure. Just to cover his tracks, he wiped the steering wheel and the door handle with his shirttail.

He walked away from the car to a hotel he'd seen about a mile away. There, he spent the night. A taxi to the Tijuana bus depot the following morning allowed him to catch a nine-fifteen bus to Mexicali.

Once there, he'd had almost an hour for lunch in Baja's second-largest city. At noon, another bus delivered him to San Amaro, getting him back home before four.

Finally home, Malcolm lowered himself wearily into his beloved recliner, exhausted. Yesterday's hangover and all that travel were part of it, he knew. But all those hours sitting on a bus, alone with his thoughts, had taken a much bigger toll on him. In moments, he wondered if he was crazy to be covering up what had been, or at least started as, an accident.

He wasn't the kind of guy who hit women. At least, not as a matter of course. There had been a few situations, he admitted to himself, where too much booze, his rampant jealousy, and a recalcitrant girlfriend had driven him to use physical force. He wasn't proud of it.

Still, he wasn't an abuser. But in the few moments of honest self-reflection that had plagued him during the trip, that was getting harder to believe. He rose from the recliner and grabbed the only hard liquor left in his cabinet, Vodka, and began numbing the unwanted thoughts.

Two hours later, he was jerked awake by the crash of his nearly empty vodka glass shattering on the tile floor.

Chapter Eleven – Present Day

Vicente couldn't find Ricardo or Julia at the station, so he called Julia's cell. She was driving when the call came through. She tossed her phone for Ricardo to answer and put it on speaker.

"I have the material cleaned for you. It's very glitzy, kind of metallic thread and shimmery. Also, there was a necklace in all that dried muck. Gold, kind of heavy, probably not something you'd wear around the house."

She thanked Vicente for the information. Ricardo closed her phone and set it in one of the cup holders. "What do you think…maybe she was out somewhere special when whatever happened, happened?"

"It's possible, likely even. What if she were here visiting, on a holiday? That could make it nearly impossible to find someone here who knew her."

Ricardo considered that for a moment. "Unless she was staying with friends here. But the location of her remains makes it more likely she either lived out in the area, or, was sstaying with friends in that area. Who else would know that the Filberts had left their house vacant?"

"Good point. Anyway, it's way too early in the investigation to start creating theories. We need to keep our minds open."

Julia had asked Vicente to text her a photo of the necklace. It might help jog memories. By the time it came through, La Chica had just stopped in front of the second property Ana Maria had flagged for them. The photo showed a heavy, linked chain with a medallion hanging from it. About the diameter of a plum, it had markings on the disk. Julia couldn't make out the details.

The next picture Vicente sent showed only the disk, which clearly showed a bust of a Greek goddess, though she had no idea which one. It was unusual enough that people might remember it.

Don and Patty Bello's house was further west from the Hovart's and a bit north. Likely a quarter mile from the Filberts. It was a large home of cinderblock and stucco construction with a matching fence outlining the property.

Two medium-sized dogs of mixed breed were romping in the yard and came to the gate to bark at Julia and Ricardo as they approached. Julia spoke soothingly to them, and they tentatively approached the police pair. After letting Julia pet them briefly, they escorted her and Ricardo to the home's front door. A rotund, balding man opened it as they reached the step.

Ricardo, though slightly senior to Julia, demurred to Julia when working with expats and almost everyone living at the Oasis was a retired expat. His English was very poor, though he'd recently started doing Duolingo semi-regularly to improve it. Julia's English fluency had been her ticket to becoming a detective in a land where female police officers were held in low esteem. She explained why they were there, and the duo was invited inside.

Patty reacted to Julia's news about a skeleton in a cistern nearby much like her neighbor. "Oh, my God." Her ample body sagged into the couch.

Julia learned the Bellos had been living in their house during winters for the past twenty years, arriving in November and staying until April. As Canadians, they needed to spend at least six months back home to retain their Canadian healthcare. Don had known Jeremy Filbert senior fairly well as they golfed together occasionally. He hadn't heard about his death sixteen years ago and had wondered all this time why they stopped coming to San Amaro.

Patty remembered Rosemary Filbert as a homebody. She rarely joined her husband when he attended the various festivals and celebrations held downtown throughout the winter months. She had met Rosemary's husband but didn't know him well.

When asked about neighbors who had lived in the area ten to fifteen years ago but had moved, they echoed Angie Hovart's reply. Yes, there had been a fellow who met those criteria, but they couldn't remember much about him.

Patty explained. "He was a bit of a curmudgeon. Never waved when we passed on the road. That kind of thing."

The Bello's house didn't have a direct line of sight to the Filbert property, but Julia still asked if they had seen any construction activity there during the past ten to fifteen years. Both shook their heads.

Julia and Ricardo left the couple with a business card and the request to call if they remembered anything that might be helpful. She also gave them the same admonishment she'd given Angie Hovart about Facebook, though she wasn't confident it would be heeded.

Since they were in the vicinity, Julia drove to Tom and Angie Hovarts, hoping to catch the husband at home. No one answered, so they headed back to the station. Discussing the case as they drove, the pair began to feel the weight of trying to investigate a decades-old crime, with virtually nothing to go on. And the frustration that went with it.

At the station, Julia's first stop was the forensic lab. She wanted to have a look at the medallion and the material Vicente had cleaned for her. As she'd expected from his description of the fabric, it was gold and silver lame. The necklace, however, was not what she'd expected.

She'd pictured it as much larger from the photos, but there hadn't been anything to show scale. Vicente apologized for not providing a ruler in the photo and remedied the problem by taking more pictures of the items with a ruler. It struck Julia that the item was about the same size as a twenty-peso coin.

Ricardo was making notes of the two interviews on a whiteboard in the war room. He printed carefully and was rewarded for his effort when Julia joined him. "Ricky, you've learned how to print legibly. Fantastic." She showed him the fabric Vicente had given her. More than ever, she was out somewhere special. This is beautiful material."

"You mean like New Year's Eve or something?"

"Or a special party, a birthday, or anniversary, maybe?"

Ricardo's phone buzzed. Dr. Serrano's name showed in the display. Ricardo answered eagerly, putting the phone on speaker.

Chapter Twelve – Thirteen Years Ago

It had been more than a decade since a hurricane had hit San Amaro, though a couple of tropical storms dumped large amounts of rain on the town in the interim. The residents of northern Baja, at least those with television or radio, were glued to the news about Hurricane Lois.

Her current path projected landfall near San Quintin, Baja, on the Pacific coast, then over the mountains to San Amaro before crossing the Sea of Cortez. It was expected to lose speed before hitting the mainland in Sonora.

Malcolm was hunkered down in his house. He'd placed sandbags outside the thresholds of exterior doors. At the last door, he placed those sandbags on a towel and threaded the end of it under the door sill. When he closed the door and pulled the end of the towel, the sandbags snugged up nicely against the outside of the door. He hoped these precautions would keep the rain from filling his house if it flowed that way.

The Oasis property sloped on a three percent grade from the mountains down to the sea. When large amounts of rain fell quickly, the water found its way to the sea by cutting channels, *arroyos*, through the sandy terrain.

It was impossible to predict where those arroyos might develop. Only one thing was certain. If the hurricane did hit San Amaro, rivers would quickly materialize to transport the vast amount of rain on its natural course from the mountains to the sea.

Hurricane Lois blew into San Amaro on winds gusting up to one hundred ten miles per hour. Trees creaked and moaned as their trunks and limbs were yanked and twisted. The sky was black long before nightfall. The rain came, and came, and came. Those living on the edges of the sea watched as the normally placid expanse became a ferocious monster, swallowing chunks of the shoreline and threatening their homes.

The power went out moments after the winds hit. When the rain began, Malcolm's sandbags helped, but some water still seeped under the doors. He spent the night running to the bathtub with a bucket of wet towels, wringing them out, and repeating the routine all night. By dawn, the rain had stopped, but water still coursed down the newly formed arroyos for another few hours.

It would likely be days before power was restored. By noon that day, generators could be heard in every area of the Oasis. Unfortunately, the cell towers that survived the storm were of little use. No power meant no phone or internet in this part of the world.

Those with four-wheel-drive vehicles drove to check on friends and neighbors. Because most houses in San Amaro had flat roofs with upper patios or, in some cases, extra living space up there, roof drainage was limited. Roof leaks were the most common damage after a storm.

Malcolm had had his roof resealed the previous year and was happy there were no leaks in the house or the garage. Some water had slithered past the sandbags outside the garage door, and a few items on the garage floor were sodden. He and his belongings had survived with minimal issues.

Several rivers of sandy water still rushed past his house. As he surveyed his property and the area around it, he watched as a sidewinder, caught by the torrents of water, struggled to gain purchase on something firm so it could escape the water. He thought about getting a shovel to try to kill the thing, but it was carried away by the current before he could.

He loaded all the waterlogged sandbags into the box of his truck for extra traction and went to check on the one thing that had been weighing heavily on his mind since the storm hit.

His heart pounded as he drove slowly past the Filbert property, not wanting to stop and risk having his truck seen there, but needing to know if their cistern was damaged. Unfortunately, due to the perimeter fence, there wasn't a clear view of the backyard from the street. He continued past the house and stopped his truck at the home of the next neighbor down the same road.

"Hey, Saul," he called out to a stooped, older man dragging a tree limb. "Let me help you with that."

He and Saul Kaplan worked together for thirty minutes to remove the debris accumulated around the house. Like Malcolm's, Saul and Martha's house hadn't suffered any major damage, mostly just debris blown about by the storm.

When he left, Malcolm said he'd continue checking on their neighbor's places. He casually mentioned that he'd already checked the Filberts and there was no damage. He got the desired response from Saul.

"That's great. I won't waste time going over there then."

Knowing that neighbors still keep tabs on each other, even those spread out in the Oasis, Malcolm spent the rest of the morning ensuring the folks in the dozen houses in his vicinity were okay. It allowed him to tell his remaining neighbors that the Filbert place was fine.

He helped those who had debris issues. Only one house had been ravaged. A portion of the ceiling in the living room had caved in. Malcolm and the owner dragged the sodden, fallen remains of the ceiling outside and shoveled them into Malcolm's truck. He promised to take it to the dump as the elderly owner had only a sedan.

Malcolm fretted the rest of the day. He prayed no other neighbor or Oasis security people had gone to check on the Filberts. That night was moonless as he walked to the Filbert house. He was dressed in black and certain no one would see him. What he saw when he got there made his heart jolt.

The metal rim and hinges of the lid from the cistern had broken and now lay inside the cistern. Shining his flashlight to the back of the tank, he could just make out the outlines of a rotting corpse through the rainwater that had accumulated in the tank.

Panic hit him squarely in the chest like he'd been gut-punched. He retched.

Malcolm needed to fix this situation, and fast.

Chapter Thirteen – Present Day

Vicente had stopped by Dr. Serrano's office on his way to work that morning and learned that the autopsy was finished. He explained what he hoped to do and was rewarded by getting the item he'd requested. Next, he'd gone to a craft store near the Malecon and bought a dozen packages of light-colored Plastina, kids' modeling clay that never hardens, a small bag of large marbles, and a couple of thin dowels.

In the forensics lab, he'd cleared a space on his worktable and laid out the recently acquired items. He'd spent hours the night before watching videos online, and now he wanted to see if he could replicate what he'd learned. He'd seen it done in person once while studying in Guadalajara.

Facial reconstruction was both a science and an art. He understood the science and hoped to be able to bring enough art to the project to make a reasonable copy of the face of the woman from the cistern.

The skeleton had been submerged in water for an extended time in sweltering temperatures. Then, as the water evaporated, the bones had been in the equivalent of an oven for an further extended period. The skull was now as clean as if it were from a Halloween prop.

Vicente already knew it belonged to a woman, so his analysis focused on discerning the features, as he'd seen in the videos. He noted the position of the cheekbones, which were a bit higher than average but not prominent, while the chin and jaw were delicate.

He did some online research on anthropology sites and decided to proceed as though the woman were of Irish descent. Natural redheads make of less than two percent of the world population but almost fifteen percent of people of Irish decent have red hair. Next, he pulled up the chart of the average depth of skin and tissue and began cutting small bits from the dowel to act as his depth markers. It took several attempts to figure out how best to attach the dowel bits to the skull.

At first, he considered using Crazy Glue. The lab always had some on hand for cyanoacrylate fuming—a technique used to lift fingerprints from porous surfaces. That idea was discarded when he considered that the skull might be needed for further analysis later. Crazy Glue would permanently bond the wood to the bone. Eventually, he opted for a glue gun. That glue residue would be easy to remove, if necessary.

It was tedious work, but Vicente was so completely engrossed in it that he didn't hear Julia and Ricardo enter the lab. Ricardo cleared his throat softly in hopes of not startling the young man. It worked. The sergeants requested an update on the forensics of the case.

"The items collected from the cistern haven't yielded any useful information. But," Vicente paused for effect. "I hope to be able to create a reconstruction of the woman's face."

Ricardo's eyebrows shot up. "I thought that was just fiction from TV shows.

"No, it's possible. I've been researching it, and I saw a demo at university in Guadalajara. I'm going to try it."

As they left the lab, Julia and Ricardo each privately prayed Vicente would successfully recreate the face of their Jane Doe. Facial reconstruction might help them determine the name of the deceased. With the name, they could start investigating from a more familiar position.

Their next stop was Dr. Serrano's office. He'd let them know he'd finished the autopsy and was compiling his report.

Vicente went back to his work. He placed two depth markers on the skull's forehead. Getting that exactly right had taken him a couple of hours. At this rate, it would take days on that step alone.

Julia dialed the number Angie Hovart had given her for Tom, who had been out when she and Ricardo went to interview the couple. A husky baritone answered on the second ring. When informed of the purpose of the call, Tom indicated his wife had mentioned they'd be calling.

But after speaking with Tom for a few minutes, it was clear he didn't have any information that could help their investigation. She was trying not to get discouraged at their lack of progress, but it felt like every idea led to nothing but a dead end.

Julia gave herself a mental shake. *This is no time for feeling sorry for myself. A woman was killed and dumped in a cistern. That's the real dead end. And it's my job to find out her story and get justice for her.*

Chapter Fourteen – Thirteen Years Ago

Based on his previous midnight reconnaissance of the Filberts cistern, Malcolm had bought a few items at the nearest hardware store and constructed a plywood and two-by-four replacement door. As he installed it with the feeble light from his flashlight, he realized he'd also need to cover the area with something more substantial. Otherwise, his replacement door would attract attention.

The Filbert property was rectangular, about ninety by one hundred feet. The house and attached garage were centered on the lot, with a perimeter fence of cinderblock. Very little had been done in the way of landscaping, meaning the yard was mostly sand. A lone ocotillo stood in one corner of the yard.

The underground cistern was at the south end of the house, abutting the south wall of the garage, right outside the back door to the house. A ground covering there would look like a logical way to keep from tracking sand into the house.

Over the next two weeks, he made a brick patio using cheap, locally made bricks. He used a simple pattern of checks, two bricks per square, alternating between lengthways and widthways. Completed, the patio was about fifteen feet square. It wasn't perfect, but it would pass casual inspection.

He was unwilling to risk having his truck seen at the Filberts, so he lugged a few bricks there each night. He loaded a half dozen bricks into each of two sturdy backpacks each night and trudged to the Filberts, a pack on his back and one in front. Each step of every journey was haunted by a nagging feeling he was being observed.

The entire time since the hurricane, Malcolm had been living on adrenaline from the fear of being caught, of Heather's remains being found, of the truth of his actions being uncovered.

In the three years before the storm, he'd overcome his self-disgust at his actions that fateful night. He'd justified them, reasoning that her lies provoked the whole thing. Plus, she did the damage to herself when she fell against the bathroom counter. He conveniently forgot his drunkenness, his jealousy, and his physical and verbal abuse that night.

Working alone in the darkness of the wee hours, trudging back and forth, weighed down by the heavy bricks and heavy thoughts, his mind played the tragic events of that night on an endless, shadow-filled loop. It wasn't long before the burden of his thoughts outweighed that of the bricks.

In addition to the sand he swept over the bricks to fill in the cracks, the patio had been christened by his tears. The first ones he'd shed for Heather. And in moments of honest self-reflection, he had to admit that many of those tears were for the man he'd believed himself to be…but no longer was.

As quickly as introspection began, however, it was swept away. More often than not these days, fury was his mind's broom. Rage was his savior—vindication, the result. If Heather, and for that matter all women, would just be faithful and loyal, he wouldn't be pressed to take drastic action to defend himself against their deceptions.

Angie Hovart had trouble sleeping. Not just sometimes, but every night. For years, her solution was to quietly slip from bed so as not to awaken Tom. She took her book to the living room and read in her favorite chair by the window until her eyelids began to droop.

That night, as she looked into the black nothingness outside the window and pondered an interesting metaphor from her book, something caught her attention. She stared at the spot for half a minute, then she saw it again. There was a light flickering in the distance, defused by several creosote bushes.

As her eyes adapted to the dark night, she realized the light was coming from somewhere near the Filbert property. Then, the light was gone. Only silence and blackness remained. Angie went back to her book.

By the time she crawled back into bed, her mind was only focused on the plot of her romance novel.

Chapter Fifteen – Present Day

The San Amaro Hospital was on a side street, a few blocks from Calle Guadalajara. More like a walk-in clinic than a hospital in the traditional sense, the one-story building housed a handful of treatment rooms, a small pharmacy, a few rooms for overnight patients, and a morgue. It was to the latter that Julia and Ricardo headed.

"Your victim was about five-three, Caucasian, in her early to mid-fifties, and has been dead about fifteen years." Dr. Serrano read from his notes before looking up at Ricardo and Julia. "From the small amount of hair we found entangled in the material left from her dress, she was a natural redhead. It's possible it belonged to whoever dumped the body, but I doubt that."

Julia glanced at the doctor to see if he was making a joke. There was a twinkle in his eyes, so she figured it was his attempt at lightheartedness. "What can you tell us about the injury to her head?" she asked.

"I was getting to that," he said briskly. The twinkle was gone.

"Didn't mean to rush you." She wouldn't apologize for asking a question any man would have asked. "We're anxious for a solid lead."

She walked a fine line in her career. Most Mexican policewomen never got the opportunities Julia's English fluency provided her, and many Mexican men were not happy about a woman being a detective sergeant. She hadn't previously detected this vibe from the doctor; perhaps he was having a bad day.

"Yes, of course you are." The doctor explained that the damage was likely caused by falling backward against a hard and angled object, such as a sharply edged counter.

The fall had fractured both the occipital condyles—the bony protrusions on either side of where the spinal cord enters the brain stem. He showed them on the skull of a skeleton hanging in the corner of his office. The victim's skull was with Vicente. The other damage was to the C1 vertebra, which was in two pieces.

"The damage to the vertebra is what killed her." He showed them the two small bone fragments from the victim's skeleton. "To do this much damage, she hit whatever it was with great force—more than just a simple fall. She could have lived for a few hours after the initial incident, but any sharp movement of the head would have caused the damaged bone to shear, resulting in instant death."

A guttural sound escaped from Ricardo, which he tried to cover by clearing his throat. *That poor woman.*

"It's impossible to say if the bone sheared and she died quickly or if death came much later, and the bone came apart as the body decomposed. Either way, she'd have had a massive headache and would have needed support walking because of the trauma to the spinal cord."

"One of her left molars is broken just above where the gum line would have been. The autopsy doesn't indicate if it was broken at the time of death, but it would have hurt a lot, so she wouldn't have left it like that for any length of time. If it occurred near time of death, it could add credence to the 'sharp movement of the head' theory. Perhaps she was struck on the left side of the head. That's all I can tell you."

"I'm not sure what I was hoping to learn," Julia said as she and Ricardo drove back to the station. "But we still don't have much to go on. We know her height and have Vicente's guess at her ethnicity, which is something, I guess. Do you have any thoughts on how we should move forward?"

"We've got to figure out who this woman is. I think if Vicente can successfully reconstruct her face, we'll finally have a foothold."

"I think we'd better have a Plan B in case he can't do it. Don't you? Let's go back to basics."

"Well, you remember what they taught us at the academy—who, what, where, when, why. We know *what* happened. She hit her head. So that is at least part of the means. But we still don't know the other four Ws. We also have no idea what the motive might be. I agree that everything hinges on the *who* part. Like you said, we're at a disadvantage until we can figure that out."

"Agreed. Let's see if Vicente is making any headway on the skull...pun intended." She snickered while Ricardo tried to hide a smile.

The forensic tech was hunched over his desk, a sea of pages arrayed over its surface. As the pair drew closer, they could see the pages were part of a technical paper on facial reconstruction. Four pages had photos showing a step-by-step reconstruction of the face belonging to an ancient skull found in Africa.

Their victim's skull sat on the desk beside all the pages, small bits of dowel attached to its surface, and a small mountain of cream-colored plastina packages behind it. Vicente had opened one package and was preparing to place quail's-egg-sized balls of the putty into the vacant eye sockets as shown in the paper. Perhaps he wouldn't need the marbles he'd bought.

"This is way harder than it looks," Vicente said after realizing who'd entered the lab.

"It looks like you've done a good job with the depth markers," Julia said, hoping to encourage him. "How do you know how deeply each part of the skull should be covered with the plastina?"

"Well, it's based on the ethnicity of the person. Dr. Serrano told me she was Caucasian, and I found naturally red hair snared in bits of fabric. So, I did some research and found that Ireland has the highest percentage of redheads in the world. I'm basing the depth markers on that." He pointed to his computer screen, which displayed several images of red-haired Irish women.

Then he clicked another tab, revealing a table of depth markers specific to Irish people. The page logo proclaimed the University of Manchester, Centre for Anatomy and Human Identification as the source. "This information has been invaluable. And thank God for Google Translate because it's all in English."

Ricardo, very curious about the reconstruction process, perused one of the pages on Vicente's workbench. Then set it down when Vicente continued.

"I reached out to one of the forensics professors I had in Guadalajara, and he told me about the work the University of Manchester was pioneering. He even gave me the name of one of the anthropologists working there in the CAHI, as they call it. I emailed her, and she's Spanish! She's already given me some great tips. She and two of her coworkers wrote this paper." Vicente tapped the pages in front of him.

"Wow, that's great. Do you have any idea how long the rest will take?" Julia asked. "It seems like we're stalled without some idea of who this woman was."

"Why don't you check back tomorrow. I really have no idea how long the next steps will take."

The pair went to update Inspector Martinez on their meager progress.

Chapter Sixteen – Twelve Years Ago

Malcolm felt zombie-like as he went through his usual routine. At times, he thought the routine was the only thing keeping him sane. He still went to water volleyball often, hosted a bi-weekly poker game with his buddies, and went to the brewery several afternoons a week.

He hadn't dated anyone since Heather 'left'. Some days he managed to banish his fears of someone discovering her body. Most days, it was a terrifying companion. It haunted his dreams and taunted his efforts at bonhomie.

The bottom line was, he was afraid of this new side of himself and what he knew he was capable of. But mostly he was afraid of being caught. It had been three years, and during that time he had not only created the falsehood of her departure but developed a detailed backstory about where she went and what she'd done in the intervening years.

He'd been inundated with questions from her girlfriends in the weeks directly after her death about where she was. He faithfully reiterated the narrative he'd written the day of her 'departure,' trying to remember to alter the words he used each time. He'd seen TV shows where groups of bad guys were often convicted because they all gave exactly the same alibi. The word-for-word accounts tipped off their interrogators.

Eventually, Malcolm suggested to those asking that she might have wanted a clean break from San Amaro, perhaps to be with someone she'd met in town. Though not overtly stated, he intimated she may have moved back to the States. After a while, they stopped calling.

This day, as he trudged through his daily routine, weighted down with self-loathing and worry, he again had the foreboding feeling of being watched. As the day wore on, his thoughts became darker.

Did one of his neighbors know? Were they watching him? Had someone seen him on any of his many visits to the Filbert property? He couldn't shake the dread.

His thoughts returned to the latest addition to his lie, where he told Heather's concerned friends that she may have left to be with a new man. This had worked well to allay people's concerns about her whereabouts. Malcolm dug out the pages he'd pulled from his spiral notebook and updated the fiction he'd written three years before to include Red's leaving to be with someone.

After rereading his story, he augmented his fiction with the notion that she might have returned to an old boyfriend in Loreto. The one she'd just left when he met her there while on a fishing trip with some buddies. Or she could be with a guy she'd met one night when she was out with her girlfriends—the guy he'd seen her with while they smoked outside.

Why not? She could easily have left me like she did the guy in Loreto. When I met her, she said she'd just broken up with him. But he called her cell phone daily for the first couple of weeks after she moved in with me. She was likely still living with him when we met.

He fondly turned his memory back to that time. In Loreto, she was bartending in the bar by the marina that he and his buddies frequented at the end of each day of fishing. They had hit it off immediately. She was sexy and pretty, and he couldn't get enough of her red hair, giving her the nickname Red his second time seeing her.

He invited her to come to San Amaro. When he was leaving, she kissed him on the cheek and whispered in his ear that she might take him up on his offer. A week after his fishing trip, she'd phoned to say she was on the road and would see him the next day.

He was hooked. She captivated him and they had months of carefree fun before— He stopped his trip down memory lane. His reminiscence had pulled him out of his paranoia and funk. But what came next in their relationship brought up too many things he had avoided thinking about.

He'd seen her talking to a guy on the Malecon during some festival. Malcolm had been overcome with a jealous rage and made a scene. Red had been furious with him. He'd promised it would never happen again. But, of course, it had.

He remembered how easily she'd left the guy in Loreto to move in with him—a guy she'd met in a bar and known for seven days. Of course, she was capable of doing it again. Doing it to him. His anger rose again.

Why couldn't women just be faithful?

As he habitually did when faced with unwanted thoughts, he grabbed his Jim Beam and drank until he forgot.

The next morning, he found the notebook pages of his fiction about Red, and after rereading them, his paranoia returned. He needed to move—to get away from this place and his spying neighbors.

Being this close to her body brought back the memory of what he'd done that night, a memory he could never outrun. Still, his final thought when that memory loop played in his head was that she'd betrayed him for the last time. She deserved it.

That day, on his way to water volleyball, he stopped by the sales office. He told the woman working there he wanted to list his place and find another one on the Oasis—he wasn't willing to abandon pools and other facilities that made the Oasis different from the other nearby communities. He told himself that once he was far from the Filbert house, the terror of being so close to Heather's corpse would pass, and only his vindication would remain.

Chapter Seventeen – Present Day

Ana Maria and Luis had been busy with their respective tasks and were prepared to give Ricardo and Julia their findings. When the two sergeants joined them in the war room, the constables had a pile of folders and papers prepared.

Ricardo was the first to arrive, his ubiquitous giant coffee mug in hand. Julia was just a minute behind, having stopped at Inspector Martinez's office to see if he wanted to attend the meeting. He hadn't.

At forty-three, Ana Maria was a mother of three and grandmother of two. She had her first baby at seventeen, just months after completing high school. Still living at home with her parents, she was able to work at her neighborhood OXXO convenience store while her mother tended to her baby. Her second and third children were born before she reached twenty-one.

By the time Ana Maria's kids all reached school age, she'd met and married the man to whom she was still married. He had accepted her children as his own, and together, they lived in a small trailer on the same tiny lot as his parents' equally tiny home. When she was twenty-eight, she'd applied to join the police and been accepted into the academy.

She was grateful that her husband supported her desire to have a job, though her time at the academy was challenging, as he was unwilling to be the sole parent while she completed her police training. Fortunately, Ana's mother agreed to take the kids for her months at the academy.

Ana Maria was hired into the San Amaro State police shortly after completing the academy and had worked there since. She hadn't had a promotion in all her years on the force. She treasured the opportunity Julia had provided her to get out of the station.

She unrolled a copy of the plat map for the neighborhood in which the body had been discovered. The Filbert property was marked with a red circle. She had written numbers beside each nearby property, and the accompanying typed pages explained the owners of each.

As Julia followed along, she realized the excellent research Ana Maria had done. Beside each number were the owners' names, contact information, and purchase dates. Ana Maria had also noted whether the residents were full-time or part-time and which places were rentals. In the cases where the property had changed hands, she provided the same information for the new owners. There were nine properties, three of which had changed ownership during the past fifteen years.

"Excellent work. This is exactly what we need," Julia said. Ana Maria beamed with pride.

"So, Luis, what have you got for us?"

Luis pointed to one of the stacks of files before him. "These are all the unsolved missing person cases involving a woman that occurred ten to fifteen years ago. There are seventeen of them".

"When I restrict it to women in the forty-five to sixty age range and those under five-foot-five, there are only five." Luis handed each sergeant a typed page containing a summary of the police file on each of the five. Then he gave them the bad news. “None of them has red hair.”

Julia and Ricardo took a few moments to read the proffered information. Again, Julia expressed her appreciation. It wasn’t his fault that none of the cases appeared related to their victim. Neither she nor Ricardo could think of anything else they needed the constables to do, so they released them back to normal duty. Both tried to cover an air of dejection as they left the war room.

The pair spent some time familiarizing themselves with the map and planning where to begin their remaining interviews of neighbors. They had already spoken with the Hovarts and Bellos, leaving five live-in owners near the Filbert home. They finally had some direction to start their investigation.

The next stop was the forensics lab. As they entered, a frustrated-looking Vicente greeted them. “My progress on the skull was going slowly. I don’t know if this is going to work. I just don’t think I have the skill to do it. I’m not a sculptor, and it seems like a necessary skill to get the facial features right.”

He showed them what he’d done. They could see the brow taking shape, and bits of the cheeks, and a chin.

“The problem is, I don’t know how to do the eyelids, the nose, the lips, or the ears. Filling in the plasticine to the depth of the markers isn’t too hard, but then making the actual facial features feels beyond me. I’ll keep working on it, but I don’t want you to get your hopes up too high.”

When they were driving to do their first interviews of the day, Ricardo startled in his seat. “I just thought of something. You know the cultural center at the north end of town? Well, they offer classes in pottery and clay sculpting. Maybe there's someone there who could help Vicente."

"Brilliant idea, Ricky."

While she drove, Ricardo called the center and learned that the sculpting teacher would be there that afternoon, at about three. They had time for two interviews before then. Ricardo navigated Julia to the home of Garth and Frida Taylor. It was south and east of the Filberts. "Ana Maria's notes say they were part-timers until seven years ago, when they became full-time residents."

Their brick home was in a style popular in San Amaro. The multicolored yellow, ochre, and gray bricks came in two thicknesses. The walls were built in layers of a repeating pattern of two thin layers followed by one comprised of thicker bricks.

Frida answered their knock and led them inside. The inside walls were not stucco, so they shared the same multicolored, patterned look as the exterior. Julia found it too busy for her taste, oppressive.

When Julia explained the purpose of their visit, the woman gasped. "So, the rumor is true. How awful. How can I help?"

"Where did you hear about it? Facebook?" Julia asked. And the woman nodded.

Julia asked about her husband's whereabouts as they preferred to interview couples together when they were in the information-gathering stage of an investigation. They learned he was in the U.S. and would be back the following day.

Julia provided the woman with their current description of the dead woman, including her height, age, and hair color. She also offered the five-year window of probable time of death, stressing the strong likelihood it was fifteen years ago.

Mrs. Taylor looked bewildered. “Oh my! That isn’t much, is it? Well, let me think.” She paused for a moment, eyebrows scrunched, eyes closed. “I vaguely remember a woman who matches that description. We were about the same age. I’d see her at water aerobics sometimes. Really, it’s just the red hair that I remember.”

The woman scrunched her eyes again, then continued. “That, and she drove an old orange Volkswagen Beetle. I thought it was so cute. I don’t know if that’s the person you’re trying to identify. I never knew her name. I haven’t seen her in at least twelve years. I tend to remember things as either before or after my hip replacement, which was twelve years ago. I stopped going to the pool for a few months after the surgery. But now that I think more about it, I suspect I hadn’t seen her for a few years before my surgery. Sorry, this probably isn’t of any use to you.”

Julia asked a few questions aimed at helping the woman remember anything else, but they elicited nothing more. She thanked the woman and said they’d be back to speak with her husband, leaving her with the optimistic suggestion that perhaps she’d remember more then.

Next, they drove to the home of Saul and Martha Kaplan. Finding no one home, they decided to head to the cultural center. They’d be a bit early to speak with the sculpting teacher, but neither had been there before and wanted to check it out.

Each of them harbored great hope that the teacher would be willing and able to help them.

Chapter Eighteen – Present Day

The cultural center was a pale yellow, two-story building just past the entrance to town. Julia and Ricardo entered a large foyer with a beautiful mosaic floor depicting dolphins frolicking in the sea. Both recognized them as Vaquita, the world's most endangered marine mammal, found only in the Sea of Cortez. Sadly, there were estimated to be only ten to thirteen left.

Ahead was a directory, near a wide set of stairs leading to the second floor. As they perused it, the duo discovered the building housed areas for music, dance, a wide range of visual arts, a library, and a computer training classroom.

The walls of the main floor housed an impressive array of paintings by famous Mexican artists, interspersed with students' works. Up the stairs, they found several classrooms. In one, they saw a half-dozen adults learning English. A look in the other rooms told them the classroom they wanted must be on the main floor.

Eventually, they found the right room. Ricardo approached the woman preparing for the sculpting class and learned she was the teacher they sought. As he explained how they hoped she could help Vicente with the facial reconstruction, the woman's expression went from curious—*What do the police want with me?*...to horrified—*A woman's skeleton was found in a cistern!*...to excited—*They want me to sculpt a face on her skull!*

"Yes, I'd be very interested in helping your young forensics man. Please let me show you some of my work."

The woman, who'd introduced herself as Araceli Pessoa, led them to a room behind the classroom. The room contained shelves made with slatted racks and housed drying sculptures. They ranged from tiny animals to life-sized busts. It was in front of the latter that Araceli stopped.

"These are all mine. If you can stay for another ten minutes, you can see the people from my class who sat for them. It's the technique I use for my teaching. Each class, I work on a bust of one of my students so the others can see how to handle the facial features. Helping Vicente will be a fascinating way to use my skills."

As the students arrived for their class, Julia and Ricardo told Araceli they would return at four-thirty and drive her to the station to meet Vicente and see the project. Since she didn't own a car, Julia promised to give her a lift home after the meeting. That would give them time to do a background check on the woman and get the Inspector's approval to allow an outsider to perform this task.

Shortly before five that afternoon, Julia and Ricardo escorted Araceli to the station. "I've never been in a police station before. It's a bit frightening." Seeing the woman fidgeting with her purse and glancing around wide-eyed, Julia whisked her upstairs. They entered the forensics lab and met Vicente. "Oh my, look at all this impressive equipment." The other three tried not to laugh.

Observing his work on the facial reconstruction, her lips twitched as she suppressed a smile. Plastino was a unique choice for the job and something she hadn't used in sculpting since she was six. Still, she admitted to him that he'd done an admirable job so far.

Julia and Ricardo left the two to coordinate Araceli's availability to help him and went looking for Inspector Martinez. They found him on the main floor getting a coffee. Ricardo grabbed one too, then they adjourned to the war room to fill him in. Martinez was interested and impressed by the facial reconstruction attempt and went with the pair to the lab to meet Araceli and see the reconstruction personally.

On their way to the sculptor's house, Julia asked for her opinion about the probability of the reconstruction being accurate enough to look like their victim.

"Given what Vicente has already accomplished using the depth markers, filling in the fleshy facial features should be straightforward. Things like lip fullness, nose shape, and eyes can be based on her ethnicity."

Julia's brows knit together. "Can you give me an example of what you mean?"

"If she were of Irish descent, the lips and nose would be thinner than average, the eyes less heavily browed. And of course, all the parts need to fit into those he's done already. High cheekbones would change the width of the nose somewhat, for example. I think the finished result will be close enough for people who knew the woman to be reminded of her."

Julia felt a glimmer of hope start to blossom. Perhaps they'd be able to solve this mystery after all.

Chapter Nineteen – Present Day

It had been a couple of days since Julia and Ricardo had spoken with Angie Hovart and Freida Taylor. Julia was certain that by now, Facebook and the gossip mill would be buzzing with conversations about the woman in the cistern. If the murderer was still in the area, he or she would likely be aware that the body had been found.

That evening, after eating a cheese quesadilla for dinner, she plopped on her couch, laptop in hand, and began scanning the local expats' sites. As expected, the skeleton was a hot topic. The idea that it was a cartel hit seemed to be the most popular theory. She considered it for a moment. It was unlikely. How would they know the Filbert place was abandoned? She could, however, understand why the theory was popular. It placed the blame on some entity outside their community. Still, it was unlikely.

Another theory was that it was Rosemary Filbert, murdered by her husband. It was fueled by the fact that the Filberts left abruptly and never returned. Julia shook her head. The skeleton was too young to be Rosemary, and she had heard the old woman's frail voice in the background when she'd spoken with Jeremy.

Julia's thoughts drifted to the killer. Had that person read these same posts? Shutting her computer, Julia closed her eyes and tried to put herself in the killer's mind. What thoughts would be going through their head when their old crime was uncovered?

Only seven miles away, Malcolm sat on his couch, eyes closed, trying to imagine what was in the minds of the police investigating his crime. When he'd read the first post from his old neighbor, Frieda Taylor, saying that the police had found a skeleton of a woman in the Filbert's cistern, his heart nearly exploded. That had been the previous day.

In the past twenty-four hours, Malcolm had managed to calm himself. Now, he considered the likelihood that anyone would suspect him to be very low. Since he'd moved to the house with the sky-blue door, he'd been cagey when asked how long he'd lived there. His answer was always to say he'd moved to San Amaro twenty-some years ago. If people chose to think he'd lived in that house all those years, it wasn't his fault.

Of course, there were his poker buddies who'd know he used to live near the Filbert home. And his nosey neighbor, Kate, but he doubted the cops would be able to piece that together. So, as he sat on his couch, wondering what the police were thinking, he was confident his secret was safe.

Julia's perception of the killer's thoughts followed a different path. What they knew about the crime was that the perpetrator had gone to considerable lengths to cover it up. First, that person knew the Filbert's place was abandoned. Who would know that?

A neighbor, security in the Oasis, the Filberts, friends of the Filberts…she racked her brain to think of who else would know. It wasn't a long list. She made a note to contact Jeremy Filbert to see if he could produce a list of friends the couple had during their time in San Amaro.

Thinking about security, her thoughts drifted back to the current prominent theory on Facebook. What if one of the security guards was connected to the cartel? That was possible, she considered, but not probable. Much more likely was that the location was picked because it was close to the killer's and known to be vacant.

A neighbor.

The killer would be shocked to learn the remains were discovered. Ten to fifteen years was a long time, enough that a person could almost have relegated the action to gone-and-forgotten. *Almost* being the operative word. A normal person, not accustomed to murder, would be hard-pressed to forget such a heinous act. Unless they were deranged or a sociopath.

That thought had her up and digging around in a box under her bed. It contained university texts that she'd kept. Finding the one she wanted, she settled back on the couch to read about mental instability. Her reasoning was simple.

If I'd murdered someone and never been caught, I think I'd go crazy with guilt and worry. Looking over my shoulder for a decade or more would unhinge me or, she thought with a start, *make me feel untouchable.*

She drifted off, wondering how that information could help with their investigation.

Chapter Twenty – Present Day

Abe Walker learned at the engineering office at the Oasis that José Amaya, the contractor he'd hired to inspect the property he wanted to buy, was on their approved builders list.

This pleased him as he'd liked the man. He spoke English well, and he already knew the issues with the house Abe had decided to buy. Jeremy Filbert had accepted his low-ball offer based on the cost of repairs, and within a month, the place would be his new home. Many of the issues with the home would need to be repaired before he moved in. Most importantly, he'd need a working cistern to provide water.

Now that the police were finished with the cistern crime scene, José had done a more thorough evaluation of the unit and informed Abe the cistern was still viable and in good shape apart from the missing hatch. His team had cleaned the remaining muck from the concrete cavern to complete the evaluation of its viability.

It had taken a morning for them to remove all the mess remaining in the tank. As a worker emptied the last pailful into the wheelbarrow, he spotted something gold in the mud and sand. After wiping the object on his shirt, he realized it was a small gold ring. Knowing of the police's interest in the bones found there, he took the item to José. When Abe was presented with the ring, he immediately dug through his wallet to find the business card Julia had given him.

Vicente, under Julia's watchful eye, cleaned the ring thoroughly. A stamp on the inside of the band indicated it was eighteen-karat gold. The top of the ring contained a pinkie-fingertip-sized emerald, around which were the words Andover High School. Julia looked at it under a magnifying glass. "Darn, there isn't a year on the ring."

Armed with pictures of the ring, Julia headed to her computer to do some research on Andover High School. She learned there were three Andover High Schools in the USA—in Massachusetts, Minnesota, and Kansas. The one in Minnesota wasn't built until 2002 and therefore was too new for their victim to have attended.

Given the age range of early-to-mid-fifties at the time of death and their time of death at ten to fifteen years ago, Julia and Ricardo estimated she would have graduated from high school sometime between 1970 and 1984.

Julia highly doubted that there would be any records from back then about which students purchased class rings. Also, she couldn't imagine phoning the school to inquire about short female redheads attending during that period. The ring might be a dead end, but Julia, ever optimistic, added the dates, high school addresses, and phone numbers to their whiteboard.

She thought about asking her cousin, Alma—the assistant head research librarian at the National Library of Mexico in Mexico City—if she'd have time to do some digging for her. But she decided that it was too soon. Once they had a name, perhaps Alma's skills would be beneficial. She shook her head and sighed deeply.

"What's wrong?" Ricardo had a serious look on his face. It was the first time Julia remembered him asking so seriously. Normally, he'd say something like, *What's up, Lucy?*

Julia feared they were losing the comfortable banter that had once formed the bedrock of their relationship. A few months ago, she and Ricardo had a candid conversation about her 'just friends' boundary with him. At the time, Ricardo had reassured her that he understood her reasons—a woman trying to climb the career ladder in the Mexican police would lose credibility if she were sleeping with a coworker.

Julia's aspirations were known. She had never been shy about saying she wanted to become the station comandante, as her grandfather had been. Ricardo understood, but he was unhappy. Julia had noticed he was more reserved around her than he'd once been. Their usual banter had dried up. It made her sad. She hoped they'd get past this soon.

"It's just my ongoing frustration that we don't have anything solid in the way of leads. No name, no idea where she lived, who her friends were, nothing. I was thinking of asking Alma to do some digging into the high schools, but we don't have anything solid enough to give her."

"Is that something Ana Maria could do?

"I did think about that, but this will involve talking with English speakers. That's why I wanted to see if Alma has time for it."

"Makes sense. Let's hope the facial reconstruction gets us somewhere." Seeing the sadness on his partner's face, he went on. "We'll get there. One way or another, something will break for us soon. Right, Lucy?"

Julia's heart caught at his use of her nickname. Perhaps the pendulum of his mood was swinging from solemn back toward their previous companionable friendship. "Absolutely, Ricky. Let's find ourselves something to propel this investigation forward," she said with more confidence than she felt.

Chapter Twenty-One – Eleven Years Ago

Malcolm was finally feeling settled in his new home. It was smaller than his old one—only two bedrooms. But it had a small room he used as an office, with a desk for his computer and room for a couple of shelving units for storage. A one-car garage on the opposite side from his nearest neighbor, Kate, housed the car he now used only for long drives and trips to the States.

The sky-blue door sat in the middle of the front of the pale-yellow house. A four-foot fountain sat a few feet in front of the door. Malcolm had needed to replace the pump to get the fountain working, but soon tired of refilling it with water every day. Evaporation was not his friend.

The interior of the place was dated. Being located in the oldest district in the Oasis, it had been built in the late eighties and hadn't been updated since. The living room walls were comprised of wainscotting bottoms and gold and burgundy wallpapered uppers. The used furniture he'd picked up at the swap meet looked garish when juxtaposed with the walls and patterned carpet.

Malcolm hardly noticed the discord in his living space. The home was close to the main pool complex on the Oasis. That was the reason he used for moving when asked. He'd repeated it so many times that he had convinced himself it was the only reason he'd moved.

That day, as he walked the five minutes from his home to the pools, he was delighted he'd made the move. Not being within eyesight of the Filbert's property and the memories it evoked was good for him. He was happier and more active. Being able to walk to the pools encouraged him to go more often. Since he'd moved into his new place, he'd become a daily player at water volleyball. He'd even noticed his beer gut shrinking.

It had taken longer than he'd expected to sell his old place. He'd eventually decided to move into a month-to-month furnished rental apartment. It was near the brewery and just across the highway from the pools.

The realtor he used staged his old house once Malcolm moved out, removing much of the clutter lying in every corner and on every flat surface. Malcolm had to admit the place looked much better after the staging.

The Mexican couple that bought it was from Mexicali. They'd been looking for a weekend getaway and wanted to buy it furnished. That was fine with Malcolm. Most of his stuff was too big for the house he had his eye on. As soon as the deal on his old place was finalized, he made an offer on the house—the one with the sky-blue door—he now called home. He'd moved in three months before and could feel his mood improve every day. He felt almost euphoric.

Inside the pool complex, the Oasis sports coordinators, a pair of young Mexicans—Rubén and Omar—were setting up the activity pool for volleyball when Malcolm ambled toward a poolside table. Ropes floating inside pool noodles formed the court boundaries—faded red at the north end and blue at the south. The net was suspended over the pool from poles inserted into specially-made brackets. A half dozen deeply tanned people were sitting around the pool awaiting the start of the games.

Malcolm said hello to those nearest the table upon which he plonked a small beach bag containing his towel and a couple of cans of beer. He popped the top on one and took a long pull. Omar, carrying a clipboard holding a pad of yellow-lined paper, stopped and asked if he was playing, then added his name to the list.

Shortly before noon, Omar tapped on the microphone to get everyone's attention before announcing the names of the players on each team. There were eighteen players that day, three teams of six. Teams One and Two were called into the pool. Malcolm was on Team Three, so he sat back with his beer to watch and heckle those playing the first game.

Glenn Wilbur, also on Team Three, wandered over to Malcolm's table with a beer of his own. Glenn, a tall, muscular Dane, sported a graying blond brush cut. "Hey buddy, when's your next poker night? I was sorry to miss the last one, but Rhonda and I were hosting the quarterly Pickleball Potluck."

Malcolm squinted at his phone for a moment and looked up, smiling. "You're in luck, Glenn, Benny just canceled. He made up the sixth spot last time and wants to be included whenever we don't have a full complement. The game's this Thursday night—Texas Hold'em—starting at seven with a five-dollar maximum bet. It'll be us, Tom, Ray, Charlie, and Chu-lee."

As he said the names, Malcolm realized they were the same five people who had been at another poker night four years before. The night he'd sent everyone home early. The night…

Sickening memories surged back into his mind about the night Heather, the unfaithful bitch, had left him. His euphoria evaporated, and a dark shadow descended over him.

Malcolm registered that Glenn was standing, looking down at him. “You okay Malcolm? You look lost in space. Team Three is up. Come on.” Glenn held out a hand and hauled Malcolm out of his chair.

It had been a while since memories of that fateful night had haunted him. It took Malcolm half the game to get them out of his head. The jovial atmosphere, physical exertion, and splashing water all worked their magic. By the second game for Team Three, Malcolm’s mind was again cleansed of bad memories, as though they’d never happened.

Chapter Twenty-Two – Present Day

Araceli worked only three days a week at the cultural center, leaving her plenty of time to assist the police with the case. On her next day off, her husband, a tile setter, dropped her off at the police station on his way to a construction site.

It was early—barely seven-thirty—so the sculptor was at the station before the day shift began at eight. Julia generally arrived between seven and seven-thirty. It was her favorite time to get ahead of email and paperwork.

When Julia entered the station's foyer just minutes after Araceli, she was excited to find the woman waiting.

"Morning." Julia motioned to the artist to follow. Together, they passed through the ground-floor area housing the constables' and sergeants' desks, coffee station, and meeting area. Armed with steaming mugs, they went upstairs to the war room.

On the way, they paused at the forensics lab, but Vicente wasn't in yet. In the war room, Araceli became absorbed by the plat map displayed on the wall—a detailed layout of properties around the Filberts. She studied the map, lingering on the owners' names.

"I've never been to the Oasis. It's nice to see Mexican names on some properties. I thought it was exclusively for Americans."

Julia nodded, remembering her same mistaken assumption. Her police work had revealed the surprising diversity in San Amaro, a tiny town that somehow managed to be cosmopolitan. "A lot of people think that." She shared what she'd learned about the mix of nationalities she'd encountered on the Oasis.

Their conversation was interrupted by Vicente's arrival. Juggling a coffee and a bag of pastries, he leaned against the doorway, smiling. "Hey, you two. I brought breakfast!" He set the bag on the table and the three dug in, enjoying a few minutes of lighthearted chatter.

"Do I smell donuts?" Ricardo's booming voice carried from the hallway. He appeared moments later, his grin as big as his appetite and coffee mug. After a round of banter, Vicente and Araceli headed to the lab to continue the intricate process of reconstructing the skull into a lifelike face.

It was meticulous work, but for Araceli, it was an exciting challenge. Her skills as a sculptor were being put to the test in a way she'd never imagined. Vicente, meanwhile, saw the task as a chance to refine his forensic expertise. Both hoped the final product would provide the breakthrough they desperately needed: a face familiar enough to jog someone's memory and finally bring a lead to the decades-old case.

While Araceli and Vicente tackled the reconstruction, Julia and Ricardo drove to the Oasis and set up at the activities pool before the day's water aerobics class. As swimmers arrived, Julia approached each one, asking if they'd attended the classes a decade or more ago and if they remembered a woman with long red hair.

Frustration began to creep in as most responses were blank stares or polite shrugs. Then the instructor arrived. The duo learned she'd been leading the classes at the Oasis for more than fifteen years and did recall a redhead attending sporadically in the early days.

Julia pressed her for details, but the instructor's memory was limited. The woman had come with friends occasionally, and sometimes a man who played water volleyball. No one's name came to mind, however. Before leaving, the instructor took Julia's card, promising to call if anything came back to her.

As Julia and Ricardo walked back to the car, their steps were heavy. Still, they couldn't shake the sense that even the faintest lead, like the class ring—if pursued with enough determination—might turn the tide on this cold, stubborn case.

Before going to the station, Julia had something else she wanted to do. She pulled La Chica up in front of the hair salon she frequented and told Ricardo she'd just be a second. Inside, she spoke with the owner, who went into the back room and returned a few moments later with a paper bag. Julia thanked her, paid, and left.

Back at the station, Ricardo and Julia rushed to the forensics lab, their earlier frustration giving way to a spark of hope. Vicente and Araceli were deep in concentration. The reconstruction was coming to life, layer by meticulous layer.

Julia reached into the paper bag to pull out what she hoped would be a game-changer. "This might help." She handed the bag to Vicente. His eyes lit up as he pulled out a long, vibrant red wig.

"This is perfect." He stepped back to show Araceli's progress. "You have to see this."

As Julia and Ricardo moved closer, their expressions shifted from curiosity to amazement. The face was no longer just a lifeless form. It had depth and personality. Araceli had sculpted eyes using the large marbles Vicente purchased at the craft store, painting them white with piercing sapphire-blue irises. She'd textured the brows with tools from her own kit and now was shaping the nose, her hands steady with precision.

"It's incredible." Julia's voice was filled with awe.

Ricardo nodded, pulling out his phone to snap a photo. "It's starting to look like someone." His tone held renewed optimism. For the first time, the thought felt real—they might actually put a name to the woman in the cistern.

Chapter Twenty-Three – Present Day

Julia rushed home from work. Her beloved cousin, Alma, had arrived from Mexico City that afternoon, and Julia couldn't wait to see her. She'd bought a chilled bottle of Chardonnay on her way from the station, knowing it was Alma's favorite. Her cousin was staying with their grandparents, just meters from Julia's own humble casita. Elda, their grandmother, had planned a homecoming feast in celebration.

Julia's home only had one bedroom with a single bed, so Alma was staying in their grandparents' extra bed. Alma was waiting for Julia as she drove into the family compound and embraced her cousin in a long hug. They went first to Julia's place so she could change. While she did, Alma told her what the menu was for the evening meal. Julia's mouth watered with anticipation.

Before heading to their grandparents' home, the two women took a few minutes to catch up. It had been a couple of years since they were last together, when they'd met in Ensenada at Alma's father's place. And while they talked on the phone regularly, being together was a special joy for them both.

The two had grown up together. Being only a few months apart in age and living nearby through their youth, they'd attended the same school, been in the same classes, and had even gone to university together in Mexicali as they got their undergraduate degrees. They were as close or closer than sisters. There'd never been the kind of rivalry between them that sisters sometimes have.

"So, are you still seeing Hernando?"

In place of an answer, Alma held out her left hand. On it was a classic, round-cut diamond in a simple gold setting. It was the perfect size for Alma's petite hand. "Oh my God, it's beautiful. Tell me everything. But first, let me open this wine so we can toast."

Glasses in hand, Alma gave Julia the details of Hernando's proposal. He'd made a beautiful meal of pozole with all the fixings. Both women knew it took hours to properly prepare. Julia's eyebrows shot up. "He cooked? I'm impressed. Tell me more."

In addition to the meal, he had set a beautiful table with a tablecloth and candles, and he had Alma's favorite music playing. "It was so romantic, Julia. I am so happy. We plan to get married next spring in Mexico City. You have to come. I want you to stand up with me."

Though Julia had been hearing about Hernando for several months, Alma was so excited that she told Julia much of what she'd already shared. Julia was so delighted for her cousin that she happily listened again to what a wonderful person he was in Alma's eyes. Julia suspected that their grandparents had been showered with much the same information in the two hours since Alma's arrival on the bus from Mexicali that afternoon.

As Alma's recital of Hernando's superior qualities wound down, Alma glanced at her watch and realized she'd been hogging the conversation for almost an hour.

"Oh goodness. I've been talking your ear off, and I haven't asked you anything about what's going on with you. Let's finish the wine after dinner. I want to hear all about what's happening in your life…including the case you're working on. From the little Papito Juan told me about it, it sounds fascinating."

The women walked across the sandy expanse of yard from Julia's casita to their grandparents' home. As they opened the door, the delicious smells of Mexican food filled the air. Elda explained that since the family was together now, and would not be for Mexican Independence Day, which was in September, they were having that holiday's traditional meal served today.

A platter containing Chiles en nogada had pride of place in the center of the table. Roasted dark green poblano chiles, stuffed with ground pork, apples, peaches, nuts, and mouth-watering spices, swam in a rich sauce of walnuts, creamed with milk and cinnamon. Edging the dish were fresh pomegranate seeds and chopped parsley. Ice-cold glasses of horchata, a sweet, creamy drink made from rice and flavored with cinnamon, sat beside each plate. Julia and Alma could hardly wait to dig into the feast before them.

Also seated at the table was Alma's dad. He had arrived while Alma and Julia were catching up. Alma was thrilled to see him, especially since she hadn't expected to see him for another two days, when she had planned to take the bus to Ensenada on Wednesday to visit him. He explained that he wanted to spend more than just a couple of days with her and that they could drive to his home together. She could still fly home from there.

As promised, after dinner and lengthy conversations, Julia and Alma retired to Julia's place to finish the wine. Julia gave Alma an overview of the case of the woman in the cistern and warned her that some Alma-research would likely be needed if she was willing. Alma agreed immediately, saying she was always happy to help.

As they said their goodnights, the two women made plans to spend another evening together with the family before Alma and her dad left for Ensenada.

Chapter Twenty-Four – Present Day

The next couple of days were frustrating ones for Julia and Ricardo. They visited the homes of several neighbors of the Filberts but learned very little. They were still pinning their hopes on the facial reconstruction, which appeared to be nearing completion. With so little progress being made and no new leads to follow, Julia didn't feel guilty for leaving early for the second day in a row.

She grabbed a bottle of merlot from her local grocery store and a couple of tamales from a street vendor on her way home. She was meeting Stella and Pippa tonight to discuss their progress on developing education programs for local police forces and school districts about human trafficking. She'd provide whatever input she could.

At her casita, she showered, changed into jeans and a blouse, and enjoyed one of the tamales before heading to Stella's house with the bottle of merlot. Her grandmother was outside enjoying the cool evening as Julia walked to La Chica. They chatted for a minute, and Julia learned Alma and her dad had left that morning. She was grateful she and her cousin got to spend time together the previous evening.

Julia explained her evening plans, kissed her abuela on the cheek, and drove to Stella's.

Stella's house was in town rather than one of the expat communities north of San Amaro. It was a cute two-bedroom home surrounded by a cinderblock fence. The inside of the wall displayed a beautiful painted mural depicting San Amaro Bay, fishermen in their pangas, and jumping dolphins. The painting hadn't been there when Julia visited Stella's home previously.

Stella and Pippa already had a bottle of wine open, and a glass was poured and waiting for Julia when she arrived. They were curious to hear if any progress had been made in identifying the woman in the cistern and were fascinated when Julia told them about the facial reconstruction that Araceli was doing.

"I had the impression from TV shows that it's a specialized skill. Is that woman—Araceli, was it—trained?" Pippa asked.

Julia told them about their forensic technician's work thus far and his inability to sculpt the face. Ricardo thought using an actual sculptor to assist Vicente would help, which led them to Araceli.

The story reinforced Stella's long-held belief that the ingenuity of the Mexican locals could solve any problem, usually in very creative ways. "I can't wait to see the finished product. I hope it gets you the identity of that poor woman."

The talk then turned to the purpose of their meeting. Pippa indicated that since their last meeting, she and Stella had connected with the Freedom Network in the US, a coalition of experts and advocates fighting human trafficking through a human-rights approach. They shared some of the resources used in their training programs aimed at law enforcement and attorneys.

Their contact at the Freedom Network also put them in touch with three agencies in Baja working to protect and assist those most vulnerable to trafficking. Julia wasn't aware of any of the groups mentioned.

Over the next hour, Stella and Pippa shared what they'd learned from speaking with people in those agencies. The areas of their focus included awareness campaigns, victim support services, and measures to protect vulnerable populations. Those groups considered northern Baja to be their area of responsibility, though they only had offices in Tijuana and Mexicali.

"Interesting that I have never heard of any of those groups. It's too bad because it sounds like they offer useful and important services. So, how do you plan to proceed with your own charity?" Julia asked.

"Well, we'd like your input." Stella described the idea of creating an office in San Amaro that could provide staff to work in conjunction with the other three Baja agencies. Concluding by saying that rather than creating a new wheel, they wanted to set up a satellite office in San Amaro, with staff and funding to support to have the work already underway. It would also likely include financial support for those agencies to develop programs that were more suited to the issues of smaller towns in Baja, like San Amaro.

"I think that sounds like a great idea. Have you spoken with any of these agencies about it yet?"

"We wanted your input before we did," Stella said. "At the very least, I know I can provide them with some funding. None of them is government-run, so I know they'll need money. However, I just don't want to fund work that's only focused on Mexicali and Tijuana. I know they make up almost seventy-five percent of Baja's population, but the rest of the state needs support too."

"Yes, do try contracting one of the existing agencies in Tijuana to develop some programs, similar to theirs, but more tailored to the needs of San Amaro. Specific education programs, like those we talked about before, focused on the police and schoolchildren. You'll also need to hire someone bilingual in Spanish and English for your office here. Someone who can interface with the other Baja organizations focused on this issue."

The three women finished the wine as they continued talking about how Stella's inheritance could best help. They hadn't reached any conclusions, but Pippa and Stella knew their next steps would be to meet with the existing groups in Baja to explore their needs and what they had to offer San Amaro. Julia, after a quick call to verify the person's availability, connected them with a local woman who worked as a Spanish-English translator.

Hugs were shared all around when Julia prepared to leave. As she drove home, she contemplated the friendship that was growing among the three. Being a police officer was not the best profession for making friends outside the force. Though Stella and Pippa were both older than her grandparents, Julia was grateful to know them and for their deepening relationship.

Chapter Twenty-Five – Five Years Ago

The normally cloudless skies of San Amaro had become overcast with high, wispy cirrus clouds the previous day, and the barometric pressure started to drop. Today, the cloud ceiling was dropping along with the barometer. Malcolm was watching the weather forecasts on his phone.

Tropical Storm Howard was due to hit Baja's northwest coast in the next few hours, bringing with it winds in the eighty-mile-per-hour range. Forecasters predicted it wouldn't weaken until it crossed the Sea of Cortez, so residents of San Amaro were bracing for a stormy, blustery night. Those in low-lying areas scrambled to dig out their sandbags, cover up their outdoor belongings, and move anything that could be swept away into garages and carports.

Malcolm, however, wasn't too concerned. He had recently had the roof of his home resealed, regular maintenance in the brutal heat of San Amaro summers. Situated on a slight rise, his house was better protected from potential flooding than some of his neighbors' lower-lying properties. Still, he played it safe, moving things from outside that could blow away or be damaged by a downpour to his garage.

As he worked, his mind drifted back to the hurricane a few years earlier—the one that had destroyed the Filbert's cistern lid. It had led to his efforts to further bury the evidence, literally and mentally. His memory of that time now seemed murky. He wondered where Heather had gone. Then remembered the shadowy form sprawled in the back corner of the cistern beside a rusted and broken metal lid.

He pictured himself gently placing Heather's body in the cistern. She'd died, he remembered. She'd hit her head. *Had she been that drunk? Had she been roofied?* He couldn't seem to recall the details. She'd fallen and hurt herself. By the time they got home, she was dead. He tried to recollect the events of that night, but only remembered he didn't want to have to navigate the Mexican process for dealing with a dead body. *Yes, he'd simply buried her in the cistern. He hadn't done anything wrong*.

Moving had been the smartest decision he'd made. He didn't need the reminder of Heather's departure from his life. Now, his days had settled into a peaceful rhythm. He loved his routine. He was a regular at water volleyball, a member of the mug club at the brewery, and like the other regulars, stopped by a few times a week to shoot the breeze with the other guys. He'd even started playing cribbage there every week. He was very content with his simple life.

Then the storm hit. Malcolm's fabricated nostalgia disappeared, fear in its wake. Winds raging. Gusts to ninety miles an hour and raindrops like bullets on the roof. The sound was deafening.

The branches of a mesquite tree on the side of Malcolm's house banged against his bedroom window. Malcolm couldn't calm himself. It sounded like someone was trying to break in. His heart rattled his ribcage like an imprisoned man trying to escape the bars of his cell. Huddled on the floor beside his couch, he gulped Jim Beam directly from the bottle.

When he awoke the next morning to clear skies and little wind, Malcolm could not remember why he was sleeping on his living room floor, though the empty whiskey bottle gave him some idea. He vaguely recalled a ghoulish dream of a zombie-like Heather trying to breach his house to attack him, but like many dreams, the more he tried to remember it, the more it wisped away to nothing.

The seven inches of rain that had fallen overnight caused havoc for some residents, but miraculously, the power had stayed on through the storm. Like most of his neighbors, Malcolm got off lightly—just a few broken tree branches scattered across his yard. As he put his lawn furniture back where it belonged, he was relieved the storm hadn't been more destructive.

As the morning passed, all memories of the previous evening and the terror he'd felt evaporated. By dinnertime, he was feeling so cavalier that he didn't even consider a drive past the Filbert's to ensure his patio was still intact.

That turned out to be a mistake.

Chapter Twenty-Six – Present Day

Sitting on the worktable in the lab was the face of an attractive mid-fifties woman. When Julia entered the lab, her breath escaped as a sigh of amazement. Ricardo's reaction mirrored Julia's when he strode in a few moments behind her. Araceli and Vicente were delighted with their responses.

"¡Esto es la oca!" Ricardo blurted out. Literally meaning 'This is the goose', using the old idiom extolling something's excellence.

Vicente was ecstatic. Not only had he gained further knowledge of how to do a facial reconstruction, but he'd made a new friend. Araceli reminded him of his favorite aunt in Guadalajara. And together they had produced something that might actually be the turning point in the investigation. He gushed about how Araceli had filled in the facial features, using her lithe fingers and a set of sculpting tools to form the delicate lips and eyelids.

"She even brought false eyelashes and makeup in today to make the face look more real. Then she trimmed the ends of some of the wig hair to add to the eyebrows. Isn't it amazing?" He was like a young boy with a new toy.

Julia remembered the necklace that had been found in the cistern and asked Vicente to place it around the neck of their reconstruction. The skull did not include a neck, so they improvised a neck from a large soda bottle wrapped in a scarf with the pendant showing just under the chin. It wasn't perfect, but it allowed the necklace to be viewed with the face. It was a unique piece and might add another component that someone could recognize.

Julia and Ricardo each took several photos with their phones to show interviewees. Then they went to see if Inspector Martinez was free to come see the results of the reconstruction. If this was able to help them solve this case, it might be a useful skill set for the station.

When Martinez followed them into the forensics lab, his steps faltered as he took in the facial reconstruction. "This is incredible." After looking closely at the reconstruction, he expressed his appreciation for Araceli's talent and willingness to assist the police. So impressed was he with the finished reconstruction that he offered to drive the artist home so he could discuss the possibility of her future assistance as cases like this arose.

Before they left the lab, however, he instructed Julia. "Bring in a professional photographer to take pictures of the face, a front and a side picture, and make them into posters. Also include an inset showing the ring." San Amaro didn't have a daily newspaper, so they'd post the photos on Facebook and around town, requesting the public's assistance in identifying their victim.

Ricardo called José Ramos, the photographer, who said he could come to the station and take the pictures within the hour. Rumors of the bones in the cistern were rampant on Facebook among Mexicans and expats alike. Ricardo rightly guessed that José would be excited to be among the first people to see the face of the victim.

While they waited for the photographer's arrival, Julia drafted a poster in English and Spanish telling people that the police were interested in speaking with anyone who recognized the face or thought they might know the person's identity.

By mid-afternoon, the posters were printed, and most of the San Amaro State policemen and women had stopped by the lab to see the facial reconstruction in person. Julia had also formatted a Facebook post in English and instructed Constable Ana Maria Verde to use the Facebook credentials she'd created on a previous case to post it to the local expat Facebook groups.

Julia's office phone number had been provided as the police contact on the posters, and everyone hoped that by the end of the day, they'd start getting responses. The atmosphere at the police station was electric with anticipation.

Officers took bets on whether the reconstructed face would produce results. A second pool was started among the more optimistic officers about what day the identification would be made. Betting on the outcome of cases was forbidden, but it still happened.

Julia and Ricardo, with a bundle of posters, headed north of town to the gringo communities, the area the locals had dubbed Gringolandia. There were stores, restaurants, the brewery, and other gathering places where they would place the posters. Constables Lucia Canul and Luis Flores were each given a stack of posters to post around town.

Hope ran high that this would be the turning point in the case.

Chapter Twenty-Seven – Present Day

When Julia checked her messages upon arrival at the station that sunny, warm November day, she had an additional four, all about the face on the posters. The first was from the water aerobics instructor, who said the face looked like the person she remembered from years ago. She added that the woman had driven an orange VW Beetle. But she still had no recollection of the redhead's name. Two others said they remembered the woman's face. However, neither knew her name.

The fourth call had Julia shaking her head. The male caller didn't leave a name, just made disgustingly lewd comments about the remains. Julia would never understand why people chimed in when they had nothing constructive to say. Worse was when they were provocative and debasing. *What possible jollies could they get from such behavior?* She rechecked the messages from the previous afternoon.

Two of the calls sounded like promising leads, and the two from that morning, though the callers said they didn't know the woman's name, were also worth following up. They might help her and Ricardo learn more about the victim and her routine all those years before. As she added the names to her notebook and the whiteboard, she remembered she still needed to speak with Garth Taylor. He hadn't been home when she'd spoken with his wife, Frieda.

Ricardo arrived at work while Julia was retrieving the messages. She followed him upstairs to give him the news of possible clues to the identity of their victim. She found him talking with Vicente in the forensics lab.

"Morning, guys," she said as she entered. "Good news! We've already got a few leads from the posters and Facebook. My next job is to call them all back."

"I'm so excited it's providing results. I'm glad I followed through on what seemed like a whim at the time. And finding Araceli has been a stroke of genius, Ricardo." Vicente could not keep the proud grin off his face. "Thank you for finding her."

Malcolm hadn't been on Facebook yet that day, and his happy anticipation of some fun in the pool was shattered when he entered the pool complex. He was met by a poster showing a close rendering of Heather's face.

It was like an apparition before him, haunting him. The hairstyle was wrong, but there was no mistaking to whom that face had belonged. A couple of the people he played volleyball with entered the aquatic center as he stood statue-like, trying to regain his composure.

"What's up, Malc? You okay?" one of the men asked.

"Yeah," Malcolm said, thinking quickly. "I just remembered I have an appointment downtown in fifteen minutes. I'll catch you next time."

He was glad he'd driven and not walked to the pools. He sat in his truck for several minutes, shivers coursing through his body. He attempted to calm his ragged breathing and bring his mind to focus on the disaster that had just struck his easy-going life. Heather's ghost was haunting him. By the time he had driven the two minutes to his house, he'd decided he needed to take a trip. He hadn't seen his brother in several years, but decided now was the perfect time.

Callum Davenport answered the phone, looking out at the early Milwaukee snow. He was glad he was leaving for the sun and warmth that afternoon. He was surprised to hear from his younger brother and surprised at his desire to come to La Paz for a visit.

"Well, brother, your timing's perfect. I'm flying there today. When were you thinking of coming down?" Callum said, a hint of excitement in his voice. "If it's soon, you can help me get the place ready for the season."

Callum relished the thought of spending some time with Malcolm. The brothers were two years apart in age and had been close most of their lives.

Malcolm planned to arrive the following day. He didn't indicate how long he'd stay. As Malcolm hung up, he tried to think through what was likely to happen now that Heather's remains had been found and a reconstruction of her face was plastered around town.

From the implication of the poster, seeking information about the woman's name, Malcolm reasoned it could take some time for the police to determine who the woman was. Her identity would not incriminate him in itself. He tried to think of the people who'd known him and Heather as a couple. There weren't many. They hadn't socialized with their friends together much. They'd both had separate friends and activities that filled their days.

As he packed, Malcolm unsuccessfully tried to think through his plan to escape. He was too addled to keep his mind focused, but finally realized he'd have plenty of time to consider during the drive south. He didn't have to know every detail yet. He could formulate his strategy over the coming days.

By the time he pulled his rarely-driven SUV from the garage and pointed it south out of the Oasis's gate, he was feeling much calmer. No one knew where he was going, so he should be perfectly safe there for as long as it took for the interest in the old bones to fade. He'd keep his eye on the San Amaro Facebook pages so he'd know what was happening.

By the time he arrived in La Paz, he believed he'd be fine.

He was wrong.

Chapter Twenty-Eight – Present Day

Julia and Ricardo spent the remainder of their day following up on the phone leads and revisiting the people they'd already spoken with in the Oasis. They hoped the facial reconstruction would look familiar to neighbors of the Filberts. Neither the Bellos nor the Hovarts, however, could recall where they may have seen her. As they were leaving the Hovarts, Angie called them back inside. She had remembered something that might be useful.

"Please sit," she urged, settling into a long-forgotten memory. "It was about twelve or thirteen years ago. I don't exactly remember the date. I was sitting in my chair here, reading, likely around midnight. It's how I try to get tired enough to get back to sleep. I noticed someone over at the Filbert's house. There was a flashlight—flicking around, then steady, then gone. I couldn't tell who it was and didn't see any vehicles around, but it was so dark I might have missed one."

Julia carefully led Angie back through the details, hoping to uncover something more, but the memory held no more clues. As they drove to their next destination, they speculated about the timing. By the time they'd arrived at the Kaplans, who had not been home when they last visited, they were working on the assumption that the lights in the night likely coincided with the new patio construction. Perhaps that would be useful down the road.

Saul and Martha Kaplan lived two roads behind the Filbert's property, though there were no houses on the road between theirs and the Filbert's. Their back and side yards were fenced in four-foot-high chicken wire supported by metal posts. A fawn-colored Chihuahua ran along the side fence announcing Julia and Ricardo's arrival.

The Kaplan's home looked more suited to a plantation in the southern United States. The house was one-story, with Doric columns supporting a deep portico that led to a massive door of oak and glass. As Julia knocked, she saw through the glass that the plantation-like feel of the house extended to the interior. A large foyer with an elegant mosaic floor awaited their entry.

"Hello, Mrs. Kaplan?" Julia addressed an elegant older woman of indeterminate age. She introduced herself and Ricardo and explained that the purpose of their visit was to talk with her and her husband about the human remains found in the cistern of one of their neighbors.

Since the Facebook post of the reconstructed face, Gringolandia—the Oasis and other much smaller communities lining the sea north of San Amaro—were abuzz with the woman in the cistern story. They were eagerly invited in, coffee was poured, and Saul Kaplan soon joined them from a repair job he was doing on an outside light fixture at the back of the house. Their dog entered with him.

Julia established that the Kaplans had lived in their home for the past fifteen years. She also learned that they knew the Filberts as occasional bridge players at their monthly games nights. When she moved the conversation on to the time since the Filberts had returned to the States, the Kaplans' memories were hazy. But when Ricardo showed them the facial reconstruction photos on his cellphone, they thought the woman looked familiar. Unfortunately, Saul couldn't place her.

Martha Kaplan, however, had more to offer. "I used to see her at the pool sometimes." She recalled that the woman often swam with friends. Occasionally, the redhead would come alone to the early morning lap swim. "She was a beautiful swimmer—not very friendly, maybe just shy. I never did learn her name, though I remember one of her friends calling her Red."

Neither of the Kaplans recalled any construction at the Filberts and were not aware of the mysteriously appearing brick patio. Julia left her card, encouraging them to call if anything else came to mind, especially if they remembered the names of Red's friends.

Their next stop was at Grant Levy and Len Webber's home, neighbors of the Filberts. Julia parked La Chica beside a battered old purple Dodge pickup she thought she recognized. The door was answered by a short, round, impeccably dressed man with dyed blond hair showing some gray at the roots. Behind him was Rick Whorton, a man Julia and Ricardo had initially met on a previous case, a close friend of Stella Monroe's.

Rick took the initiative to introduce the police officers to his friends and explained to Julia that the three were heading to this month's Plumeria Club meeting. At this, Julia remembered seeing Levy and Webber at a Plumeria Club meeting she and Ricardo had attended on a previous case. Knowing their hosts had somewhere else to be, she got right to the purpose of their visit.

Julia soon gathered that the shorter, livelier one, Grant, led the relationship's social dynamics. Len—tall, and slender, with doe eyes and a slight stoop—busied himself clearing away brunch dishes from their kitchen nook and looked visibly upset by the idea of human remains in a nearby cistern for more than a decade.

When Ricardo showed the men the photos of the facial reconstruction, Grant immediately said he didn't recognize her.

"Oh, you remember her, Grant, you senile old fairy." Len smacked his husband lovingly on the shoulder. "Everyone called her Red. She came to our neighborhood barbeque once, with some scruffy old dude—long wispy gray hair in a ponytail and a scraggly gray beard. I don't remember his name, but he used to live somewhere around here. I don't know where. I didn't like him much, but she was a hoot."

Julia was initially encouraged, but quickly realized that neither Len nor Grant had any other knowledge of the woman they knew as Red or her scruffy companion, apart from a more detailed description of him. They placed his age at that time in his mid-fifties. He was five eight or nine and weighed in the 150 to 160 range.

As they wrapped up, Rick escorted Julia and Ricardo to La Chica. "Stella said you have been extremely helpful to her and Pippa in framing how to proceed with their charity. They're lucky to have you as a resource. Thanks for giving them some direction. Good luck on your case. Must be like trying to find the proverbial needle."

On their drive back to the station, Julia told Ricardo the full turn of phrase. "Why would someone put a needle in a pile of hay?"

That's the trouble with idioms. They don't make sense in a different culture or language.

Back at the station, Julia flipped through her notebook to find Jeremy Filbert's email address. She sent him a photo of the facial reconstruction, asking if he recognized the woman.

Next, she went looking for Luis. She had an idea.

Chapter Twenty-Nine – Present Day

"Luis, I'd like you to go back through the missing person cases from ten to fifteen years ago that match the same criteria you used last time. But this time, look for cases that have been closed." Julia had received Inspector Martinez's okay to conscript Luis and Ana Maria for another day's research.

She and Ricardo had been commiserating over the fact that people recognized the face, so it was a good depiction of their victim, but no one knew her name.

Julia explained that Red's friends were likely surprised when she suddenly wasn't around anymore. Perhaps one of them filed a report with the police.

"Then why wasn't there an unsolved case when Luis looked the first time?" Ricardo countered her theory.

"Well, someone killed her," Julia said. "And that person knows she isn't just missing. Maybe the killer made up a story about where she'd gone and told any friends who inquired. Whoever filed the report could have believed the story and told the police that she wasn't missing after all—and the case was closed."

"I don't know, Julia, it seems like a long shot."

"Don't completely discount it. What is there to lose? Luis is the one doing the work."

"I can't argue with that. I'm just saying that there are a lot of ifs and maybes in your theory."

Because she was already a member of most of the expat Facebook groups as Maria Green, Constable Ana Maria Verde was asked to start scraping posts from those groups that matched Julia's outlined criteria.

The buzz through San Amaro about the woman in the cistern had exploded when the reconstructed face was posted. Julia optimistically hoped they'd get closer to finding a name for the face and thought they'd be closer to achieving that goal if they could identify some of her friends through Facebook.

Ana Maria didn't speak or read English, but Julia had developed a process for Ana Maria. She would locate posts with certain English keywords, scrape them into a file, run them through a translator, read the posts in Spanish, and summarize her findings in a report for Ricardo and Julia. It had been a successful method on their previous case, and Julia hoped they'd get lucky again.

With the constables assigned their duties, Julia busied herself by calling the people who had left messages on her voicemail about the face on the poster. Several people provided the name Red, which was no longer news, but one woman provided the first new clue. She remembered the woman, Red, as a friend of a friend of hers. Julia and Ricardo said they'd be at the woman's home in twenty minutes.

Laurie Graham lived in the Oasis, in a condo fronting the golf course, and met the sergeants at her door, wearing golf attire. She was about five feet two, with a rounded middle that Julia had recently heard described as the 'likes chocolate cake' body. She had a plate of oatmeal raisin cookies and a pitcher of iced coffee waiting for them.

The two-story condo floor plan matched one Julia had visited on a previous case. The ceiling of the living room into which she and Ricardo were ushered towered above them, giving the already large room a grandiose feel. The view from the bay windows was the fairway for the second hole of the course.

With beverages in hand, Julia began exploring what this woman knew about their victim. As her story unfolded, the pair learned Laurie had a close friend, Mona Richardson, who had lived in San Amaro until about eight years ago when she and her much older husband returned to the States for his medical care.

Another of Mona's friends was Red. Laurie had met her only a few times and didn't claim to have known her well. "We were friendly, but not friends, if you know what I mean," she said as a preamble to the relevant information she possessed.

"Her real name was Heather, but I don't have any idea what her surname was. If I ever knew it, it's long forgotten," she said, tapping her forehead. "The last time I saw her was at Mona's fiftieth birthday party. So that would be…" She paused and did some mental math. "…fifteen years ago. There were four of us: Mona, me, Heather, and Kim. We went out to dinner and then went to the old Cha-Cha Club. Do you know the place I mean?"

Julia managed to keep her lips from twitching as she remembered some wild nights she'd spent in the Cha-Cha Club in her early twenties. "Yes, I know the place you mean. Please continue."

Laurie summarized their evening, recounting meeting four men on a motorcycle trip in Baja and partying with them until the club closed. The details were slim. Julia led her through the information again and noted the names of the other women at the birthday celebration and their contact information, learning that Kim, who was older than the others at the party, had passed away the previous year.

One other name came out on the second telling, Dutch. He and Heather had hit it off, dancing exclusively with each other for the evening.

Julia asked if Laurie thought there was any romance between Heather and Dutch. Laurie seriously considered before replying that she didn't get that impression. "None of the guys had that coming-on-to-you vibe. That was one of the things that made it such a fun evening. We just danced and had some fun. Nothing more."

Julia relayed Dutch's name to Ricardo with the notion that he may be a possible suspect. She probed the woman's memory of the men and Dutch in particular and learned he was in logistics with some big company in Denver. She added that he was younger than Heather, so he might still be working.

As they finished their coffee, Julia asked if Laurie had any pictures of the evening that included Heather. The woman scanned her phone's gallery for several minutes. Finally, her face lit up. "I do!" she said holding the phone out to Julia and Ricardo.

The picture, taken in the club, was a candid photo of four people at a table covered with empty shot glasses and beer bottles. Only one person was looking at the camera—a tall, handsome blond fellow in a plaid shirt. He was smiling and holding up his beer in a toast to the photographer.

Beside him, with flaming red hair was a woman in a gold and silver lame dress—that same material that had been collected from the cistern. Julia recognized the inside of the place in a rush of memories. The picture wasn't great, but Julia asked Laurie to send it to her anyway. She wanted to use her magnifying glass to see if the ring and necklace were also visible.

"I don't know this man's name," Laurie said, pointing to a balding man at the end of the table, "but this is Heather, and the hunk beside her was called Dutch. The one with the plastic tiara is Mona."

"Are you still in touch with Mona?" Julia asked, hopefully.

The other woman shook her head, saying they hadn't connected in several years. Julia thanked their host. They were another inch forward in their search for the full identity of the woman in the cistern. It was slow going, but it was progress.

When she returned to the station, Julia dug a magnifying glass from her desk and loaded the photo Laurie sent her on her computer. "Ricardo, come look at this. Does that look like the same necklace we found in the cistern?"

"Yeah, I think so. The photo quality is pretty crappy, but it's the same shape and size. And her dress is definitely the same glitzy material Vicente has in the lab."

"We could well be looking at our victim shortly before her death."

Chapter Thirty – Present Day

The more Julia thought about it, the more she realized that having a first name was a big step forward. She decided it was enough to have Alma start researching the two Andover high schools she'd found from the class ring. Julia told her about the progress they had made on the case, and Alma was delighted to hear from her.

Alma promised to give it her best shot but cautioned Julia not to get her hopes up. From previous research into old school records, she'd learned that data management varied from woefully inadequate to not terrible, but incomplete. Also, Alma confessed she was up to her eyeballs in a research assignment that required her to work overtime. She'd get to the schools tomorrow. Julia thanked her profusely.

One of the major challenges Julia faced when investigating a crime involving the expat community was that she was the only fluent English speaker on the force. The majority of gringos living in San Amaro were retired and living in Mexico for the affordable amenities and relaxed lifestyle. Learning a second language was not a priority for most of them.

Alma had been approved as an English-language researcher by the station commandante. She was the ex-commandante's granddaughter, worked for the preeminent Mexican research library, and, like her cousin, Julia, she spoke perfect English.

Julia decided to try to locate Mona Richardson, the birthday girl, after whose party Heather may not have been seen again—except by her killer. She hoped she'd learn their victim's full name and more information about where she'd lived.

She checked with Laurie Graham, but she didn't have any idea where Mona lived or her contact information. Julia's next search involved Facebook, but of course, there were close to one hundred people with that name. And Google was worse.

Then she thought of LinkedIn. It was not an app she'd ever used, but she'd heard that people often included more personal information there than on many social media sites. She set up an account and began searching.

Not being familiar with the app, Julia stumbled through and eventually found a few Mona Richardsons whose ages were in the right range, given that she turned fifty fifteen years ago. Most people didn't list their age, but looking at work history provided a pretty good idea of a person's stage of life. She sent a message to each one asking if they'd ever lived in San Amaro.

Next, she went in search of Ana Maria to check her progress with Facebook conversations about the woman in the cistern. The constable was just printing her summary of relevant posts. Julia gathered the names of a few people who were Facebook friends with Laurie Graham or spoke of Mona as a friend. It was a good place to start. She decided to make contact with them once she found out what, if anything, Ricardo uncovered.

Ricardo was in the records storage area with Luis, helping him review the solved missing person cases. By the look on his face, they weren't having much luck. He followed her to the war room and plunked himself down in a chair across from her with a deep sigh.

"We've got to get our records digitized. Having to search through musty old file cabinets and mildewed files, too many of which are misfiled and or mislabeled. It's impossible!"

"No luck, then, I take it."

Ricardo shook his head and explained that Luis was dutifully continuing the search, but that he needed a break. Julia mentioned that her cousin was researching the Andover high schools to see if she could find a red-haired Heather.

She handed him a copy of Ana Maria's report and suggested they both tackle the job of finding the flagged people on Facebook and searching their friends list to see if any of them were connected to Mona or Laurie Graham.

By the end of the workday, they had a list of seven people they thought might have known some of Heather's friends. Tomorrow, Julia would reach out to them. She planned to include photos of the reconstructed face and Laurie's photo from the Cha-Cha Club.

Julia headed from the war room to her desk downstairs in the open-air space where constables and sergeants had their workspace. There was a discussion underway with a knot of officers. As Julia passed them, she realized they were talking about the betting pool on whether the facial reconstruction would help them find their victim. The group was divided. She considered leaving them to it but decided to weigh in.

"Several people have contacted me saying they recognize the woman, and a couple remember her nickname, and we have a few leads. Does that count as having produced results? I seem to remember that was the basis for the pool," she said as she passed. Her remarks appeared only to fuel their debate.

She shook her head before heading to her desk to sift through the contents of her inbox. Before she left the station, she phoned her grandparents to see if she could bring home dinner for them to share. Her grandmother said no, she'd been cooking all day and had food that needed to be eaten. Julia was invited to join them. Her abuela instinctively knew when Julia needed to discuss a case with her grandfather, Papito Juan.

Tonight was one of those nights.

Chapter Thirty-One – Present Day

Juan Perez, Julia's grandfather, had been the San Amaro State police comandante, and though he'd been retired for almost ten years, he was still occasionally consulted by the current comandante on particularly difficult cases. Julia, therefore, felt no qualms about seeking his advice on her own cases.

Even before she had attended the police academy, Papito Juan had begun sharing interesting and unusual cases with his granddaughter to gauge her aptitude for policing. He found her an avid student with a bright mind.

He was very proud of her and her success. Being a woman police officer in Mexico was difficult. Many male officers didn't believe women should be cops, claiming they should be homemakers and mothers first. Women couldn't be trusted to put the job first, at least some male officers felt that way.

Julia's commitment to her profession could not be faulted, and her success in handling difficult cases had earned her the respect of many, but not all of her fellow officers and the station commandante. When his wife told him Julia was coming for dinner, he knew that after eating, they would retire to the roof and discuss her current case. He relished the opportunity to hear more about the woman in the cistern.

After a delicious dinner of cheese enchiladas with tomatillo sauce, Julia helped clean up the kitchen, and then she and Juan retired to the rooftop deck. The night sky was transitioning from deep purple to black, and the stars were bright against their velvet background.

She began as he'd taught her by giving him an overview of the case. She explained the few clues they had so far. He'd already seen the photos of the facial reconstruction but hadn't yet heard they had the first name of the victim and a high school class ring. She told him that Alma was going to try finding a red-headed female student named Heather at one of the two schools. It was a long shot, but worth pursuing.

"The main trouble we have is not knowing the full name of the victim or a narrower time of death window," Julia said. "Five years is a broad range. However, there's a good chance that her death occurred fifteen years ago after a birthday party which the victim attended. The problem remains that it's a challenge to get people to remember things from fifteen years ago."

She told him all the avenues they were working on, then asked what else they should be doing.

Juan was quiet for a long moment. Julia wondered if he was going to answer at all. Then he leaned slightly forward. "It's a difficult case. No question. And you must prepare yourself for the possibility that it won't be solved. But let's think about what else you can do. Was there any viable DNA from the bones or teeth?"

Julia shook her head, thinking how degraded the bones were. "Dr. Serano said there wasn't any from the bones, but I don't know if they checked the teeth." *Would it even be possible now that the skull formed the basis of the facial reconstruction?* She made a mental note to check with him the next day.

Juan also mentioned that the US had several databases for forensic odontology. It was no longer essential to know the person's dentist to learn a lot about the victim from their teeth. Remains of dental work could also help them narrow down where their victim was from, though the analysis required equipment not available in San Amaro.

Juan acknowledged that during his leadership of the local state police detachment, San Amaro had still been aligned with Mexicali and able to send items for analysis to their much better-equipped forensic lab. Now, with San Amaro recently becoming its own municipality, the Mexicali lab prioritized San Amaro requests to the bottom of their list.

When San Amaro was part of the Mexicali municipality, their high solve rates bolstered the stats of the Mexicali detachment of force. Now, however, that high solve rate was viewed as competition for limited funds. It was petty, but the Mexicali force was as unhelpful now as they had been helpful in the past.

“So, if you want to get access to mass spectrometry now, you may have more success going further afield. Perhaps you could try Tijuana.”

Dental analysis to determine background was a line of inquiry Julia had not thought of, and it made her realize she had just assumed the victim was American. What if she were Canadian or British? Would that make a difference to their investigation?

Juan admired his granddaughter’s dedication to her work, but also worried that she didn’t have enough outside interests to keep her balanced. Some of that was guilt over his own hyperfocus on his career.

He hadn’t been the kind of father he wished he’d been. He was never home. He knew Julia’s mother, his daughter, suffered from his lack of presence. He was delighted to hear about Julia's involvement in Stella's budding charity.

Later, as Julia climbed into bed, her brain was busy thinking of next steps she and Ricardo could take to learn the identity of their Jane Doe or rather Heather Doe.

Chapter Thirty-Two – Present Day

Julia continued to speak with everyone who had left her a voicemail from the posters and Facebook posts. Ricardo and Luis continued to pore through ancient files, but so far, none of these avenues was providing the needed results. For the first time in her career, Julia had the unsettling feeling they might not be able to solve this murder. It had begun to gnaw at her confidence.

Then, as though the universe decided to respond to her, the answer came. Not just from one source, but several. First, Ricardo and Luis burst into the war room where Julia was returning calls from the voicemail messages. Luis proudly slapped a ratty old file folder on the table. The two men said nothing but looked from the folder to Julia as a dog to its owner holding a bone.

She was about to open it when her cell phone rang. It was Alma. Holding up a finger to the men before her, Julia grabbed the phone, leaving them to twitch in frustration. After listening for a couple of moments, she thanked her cousin and hung up, a broad smile brightening her face.

Looking up to see the people before her waiting impatiently for her to look at the file, she guessed they'd found the holy grail of their search. Rather than spoil their triumph with her news, she opened the file and saw a photo of a face very similar to the reconstruction. Julia smiled. The file contained the name her cousin had just told her.

Heather Holstaff.

Finally, they could start a real investigation.

They were so excited by their long-awaited discovery that the three spontaneously and exuberantly shared high-fives. During this celebration, Inspector Martinez and Ana Maria entered the room. Ricardo explained that they had finally discovered their victim's full name.

Martinez stepped out for a moment and returned with Vicente. With the team assembled, he praised their determination and teamwork and asked Vicente to let Araceli know the facial reconstruction had helped achieve that goal. He left the group with the next challenge. "Good luck with finding the killer."

Ricardo slipped out of the war room and headed downstairs. He went directly to the front desk, where Sergeant Zardoya was the desk sergeant on duty. Ricardo knew that he was holding the money in the optimists' betting pool.

"Hey Gustavo, we just found out the name of the woman in the cistern today. Heather Holstaff. So, who won that pool?"

The answer sent Ricardo hurrying upstairs.

Ana Maria heard Ricardo comment on the betting pool as she passed the war room door after having said see-ya-later to Vicente. Her mood perked up again as she stuck her head into the war room. "So, who won?

Ricardo beamed at her. "You did."

Ana Maria placed her report of people posting about the woman in the cistern who appeared to know her on the table. Her feeling of accomplishment was diminished slightly, knowing her work had likely been in vain since they now knew the victim's name. But she had just won some money in the pool. The thought made her grin widely. As Julia reviewed the solved missing person file Luis had found, Ricardo perused Ana Maria's report.

Julia was the first to speak. "It was Mona Richardson who reported Heather missing. In 2010."

Ricardo looked up from the Facebook report. "Great. Mona's another missing person. I mean, we don't know where she is. At least there are several people noted in Ana's report. Maybe one of them will know where we can find Mona."

Once Julia had finished reading the missing person file a couple of times, she decided to pull out the relevant information from the file. Sliding it across the table to Ricardo, she purposefully stepped to a clean whiteboard and wrote as Ricardo read to her.

Heather Holstaff

- Reported missing on 10/14/2010 by Mona Richarson
    - Contact info for Mona is local phone & address
- Last known alive evening of 10/8/2010
- Last seen in the company of Malcolm ? (boyfriend – last name unknown)
- Case closed 10/18/2010 (as solved)
- Resolution listed: left San Amaro

The phone number Mona had listed on the report had a six-eight-six area code—it was a local San Amaro number. Mona now lived in the States, so that wouldn't help. However, they also had the address where Mona had been living at the time she filed the report. They could start there.

But first, Julia phoned Ana Maria and asked her to go over her previous research into property owners near the Filbert's to discover if someone named Malcolm had lived in the area in 2010.

Mona's old address led them to one of the smaller communities in Gringolandia. All the homes fringed the beach and were a mix of small weekend getaways and palatial homes with fully landscaped yards, with a few filling the middle ground literally and figuratively. Mona's previous home was on the smaller size, but still very nice.

The current owners were strapping golf bags to the back of a golf cart as the pair of sergeants stopped in front of the house. After Julia explained why they were there, the couple introduced themselves as Millie and Frank Corbel and disappointed them by stating they'd only owned the place for six years.

After a couple more questions from Julia, Millie provided the encouraging news that they knew the person from whom they'd purchased. He lived next door. The four went to the home together and Millie introduced the police to Vikram Bharmal. Who, upon hearing the purpose of their visit, invited Julia and Ricardo into his home, using perfect, if rather oddly accented Spanish. Ricardo tried to hide a grin.

Being slightly senior to Julia, Ricardo always led interviews with Spanish speakers. He went straight to the main issue. "Did you buy the house next door from Mona and Gary Richardson?"

"Yes, I did."

"Do you have an email address or phone number for Mr. Richardson?"

"Only the one I used back when I bought the house. It might not still be good, but here it is."

"Detective Garcia, do you have any other questions for Mr. Bharmal?"

"Do you happen to have a copy of the sales agreement?"

After rifling through a file cabinet for a couple of minutes, he provided them with the requested document. Julia wrote out a receipt for the pages and promised to return the sales agreement when they had finished their investigation. She hoped it might contain more information about where the Richardsons had moved.

When the two climbed into La Chica to head back to the station, they had hope they'd finally be able to speak with Mona.

Chapter Thirty-Three – Present Day

Detective Inspector Martinez had closed his door earlier in the day to give himself some quiet time to finish a report due to the comandante the following morning. He was just reading it through a final time when a firm knock sounded. On asking the knocker's identity and learning it was Constable Luis Flores, he admitted the young officer with a pique of interest.

Luis had been in the inspector's office once before, but he had been very stressed then and hadn't observed his surroundings. Luis was feeling stressed again, but that feeling was coupled with hopefulness. The room was sufficiently large to house a desk and a small round table with three plastic chairs. It was to these chairs that Martinez directed the young constable.

Martinez had interacted with Luis several times and was impressed by the young man's dedication and ability to think through problems and develop creative solutions. "What can I help you with today, Constable?" he asked once he and Luis were seated.

Luis had been thinking about the purpose of this meeting for weeks. The recent events of the woman in the cistern case he'd been involved in had coalesced this thinking into action. "I want to discuss the possibility of me becoming a detective constable." He looked expectantly at the older and much-revered man.

Martinez leaned back in his chair and considered the request. His first words were encouraging. “Good for you, Luis. I’m glad you are considering advancing your future with the police.”

Luis’s confidence was bolstered and he relaxed slightly. The inspector reviewed some of the cases on which Luis had shone. The first was a robbery that Luis had worked on with Julia a few years before. Because of Julia’s involvement in another case at the time, Luis worked several angles of the case with minimal oversight by Julia, and both she and Martinez had been impressed by the young man’s initiative in ferreting out leads.

Next, he recalled another notable situation Luis had handled with intelligence and finesse. The comandante and Martinez, following information Luis had provided them, partnered him with another young constable. One who was suspected of selling police information to the highest bidder. Luis’s insights and actions directly aided in the arrest of that constable and his accomplice-brother.

The inspector, upon finishing his recital of Luis’s accomplishments, outlined the process of gaining a promotion into the detective ranks. The station did not currently have any detective constables, which was in Luis’s favor. There was a requirement of experience in service, most often measured by years on the force, but which could also include the level of responsibility during those years, giving Martinez some leniency if Luis’s legacy was insufficient to meet the years-hurdle.

There was a need for training and certification that he could meet through a mix of online and evening classes. The final requirement was passing the detective exam. While Luis had found most of that information from the website of the Baja Norte State

Police headquarters in Mexicali, he was interested in hearing about Martinez's discretion in certain aspects of the process.

When he left the inspector's office, Luis had a plan that he and the senior officer had developed. If he could manage regular progress in the required classes over the next year, Martinez promised to give him opportunities to work more directly with Ricardo and Julia on cases spotlighting the need for detailed detective work. The detective exam was offered four times a year. Luis knew it was up to him when he felt he was ready to take it.

A huge smile crossed his face as he trotted downstairs to his desk. He and Rosa could finally start a family. They'd met shortly after Luis first became a policeman in Mexicali and married when he was hired in San Amaro. The starting wage for a new police officer in Mexico was low—the equivalent of about $900US a month. Though his wages had increased slightly in the four years he'd been a policeman, becoming a detective constable would greatly improve his earnings.

He stood a bit taller knowing Martinez supported his bid to become a detective, meaning his place on the San Amaro force was secure. At least as secure as possible. Perhaps he and Rosa could find a bigger house to rent—one with two bedrooms and maybe even running water. He stood taller, took a deep breath, and smiled at the thought.

But first, he had much to learn and a test to pass.

Chapter Thirty-Four - Present Day

Callum was starting to wonder why Malcolm had come for a visit. Since he'd arrived, his brother had hardly spent any time with him, preferring the company of the patrons of Miguel's Cantina, a shabby bar reached from a trash-ridden alley and frequented by the neighborhood's less desirable gringos. His brother had been moody, depressed, and drunk most of the time since he'd reached La Paz.

In their youth, Callum and Malcolm had been so similar in looks that they were occasionally confused by the parents of their friends. As they reached adulthood, however, distinguishing them became much easier. Callum, at six feet, had a couple of inches on Malcolm. He also kept his hair trimmed in a no-fuss crew cut, while Malcolm had a ponytail from the time he left high school. Their facial features still shared many similarities, but because of his hard drinking, Malcolm looked years older than Callum.

Callum was waiting for Malcolm when he dragged himself out of bed. He handed his brother a sugary coffee and pointed to the couch. "We need to talk, Malc. Now."

Malcolm took the coffee mutely but sat as he'd been bidden. His head hurt, and his heart pounded. He hoped his mind was clear enough to navigate this conversation. The caffeine and sugar were helping, but he hadn't yet looked at Callum.

The situation reminded him of a time after a truant officer stopped by their home investigating a pattern of Malcolm's absenteeism. Callum, freshly graduated from high school, had sat Malcolm down and given him a hard time. He ended his lecture by strongly advising him to focus on his schoolwork. It was the only time Callum had played the big-brother card. Until now. Malcolm steeled himself for the coming talk.

Ana Maria was slightly out of breath when she pushed through the war room door. Her face was flushed, and her eyes were twinkling. Proudly, she placed a sticky note on the table between Ricardo and Julia. On it was a single word—Davenport. "It's him," she said. "He used to live less than a quarter of a mile from the Filbert's place. Malcolm Davenport."

Ana Maria explained that she'd just texted them the address of Malcolm's old property, including the names and contact information of the current owners.

"Malcolm still lives at the Oasis, near the swimming pools on the mountain side." She slapped another sticky note on the table with Malcolm's current address and phone number.

Julia thanked Ana Maria profusely as the older woman stood a little more erectly as she left the war room.

Julia wanted to know more about Heather before speaking with Malcolm. Her spidey sense told her he would be an important witness and possibly much more than a witness. Information would be her armor and weapon if he were, as she suspected, more than a witness. She was also very curious about Dutch, Heather's dance partner from the fateful night that, since finding Mona's missing report, they now believed had been Heather's last.

Julia's first action was to try the email of Mona's now deceased husband they'd gotten from Vikram. As she feared, an immediate response from the Mail Delivery Subsystem told her the email was no longer active. The phone number Vikram provided, however, was still good. When she heard voice mail kick in after five rings, she hung up. She wanted to speak with Mona, not to leave a message. She'd try again shortly.

"What's going on, Malc?" Deep lines permeated Callum's forehead. "I'm worried about you. You have something on your mind, and it's eating away at you. Talk to me, bro."

Malcolm had been fearing this conversation. His brother knew him well, perhaps too well. He knew he'd have to keep his story close to the truth. He'd never been successful at lying to Callum. He took a deep breath and put on his best poker face.

"I had this live-in girlfriend a while back. She was a bit crazy, but that can be fun." Malcolm smiled. Callum didn't return the smile. "For a while, anyway. She took off, left San Amaro, and I haven't heard from her since. But she came back to town last week and word got back to me that she was telling everyone I had stolen a bunch of her stuff and that she was 'going after me to get it back'." He used air quotes.

Callum's head dropped in frustration. He stared at his clenched fists in his lap.

"What she left at the house were a pair of jeans and a bunch of Neil Diamond CDs. I gave them to the second-hand store. They're long gone. I figure she'll give up when she can't find me. So, you've busted me. I'm down here hiding from a woman. What a coward, eh?"

Callum simply looked at his brother for what seemed like an eternity. Finally, he leaned back and sighed. "Well, I call bullshit on that. If that's all that's going on, you wouldn't be at the bar every day drinking yourself into oblivion. When you decide to be honest about what's eating you, I'm here." He rose wearily, shaking his head as he left the room. "I just want to help."

Chapter Thirty-Five – Present Day

"This is Mona," a bright voice said. Julia smiled and gave Ricardo a thumbs-up. She explained to Mona who she was and that she was calling to learn more about Heather Holstaff.

It took Mona a moment to respond. And when she did, her voice had notes of surprise and sadness. "Oh, it's so awful! I just saw on Facebook that her remains were found recently and that she's been dead all this time. What can I do to help?"

Julia reminded Mona that she'd filed a missing report on Heather in October of twenty-ten, then revised the report a few days later, saying she wasn't missing. "Perhaps you can start there. What caused you to file the report initially, and then why was it updated to solved?"

Mona told Julia about her birthday party, that Heather was one of her group for dinner, then partying at the Cha-Cha Club. She mentioned she and her friends were joined by a group of guys returning home after a motorcycle trip down the Baja.

"Yes, Laurie Graham mentioned them as well. What can you tell me about the evening?"

Mona relayed a story initially similar to Laurie's, but then went further. "Heather and a big blond guy hit it off right away, and he and his buddies eventually joined our table."

"Did it look serious between Heather and the blond man?"

"No. All they did was dance together. I think they went outside to smoke a couple of times, but I didn't get any romantic vibe from either of them."

"What else can you tell me about the fellows who joined you?

Mona was silent for a few moments before speaking again. "Well, I believe Heather's friend's name was Dutch. He was tall, with chiseled features, and blond. Oh, and I remember that he worked in logistics, in Denver, with the state government. I only remembered because my husband had also been in logistics."

Julia felt the woman had more to say, and waited.

"Heather and he danced together most of the evening and they went outside a few times together. But I can't tell you much more about him, I'm afraid. He left with his buddies just before we all headed out."

"We closed the place and, as we left, Malcolm met Heather at the door. The plan had been for me to give Heather a lift home because Friday night is when Malcolm hosts an all-night poker game. Heather was surprised to see him. She said something to the effect that his poker buddies must have left early."

"Did you see Heather again after that?"

"No, that was the last time I saw her. I called Heather two days later, but the phone went directly to voice mail. The same thing happened every time I phoned her over the next few days."

Julia could hear a huskiness enter the woman's voice. Sadness tinged her next words.

"Red always had her phone turned on. Always!" Mona was emphatic. "So, after five days of that, I got worried. I didn't know Malcolm except to say hello, so I had no idea how to get hold of him. That's when I decided to tell the police she was missing."

"What caused you to tell them she was no longer missing?" Julia asked.

Mona explained she'd run into Malcolm in a grocery store a few days after she'd filed the report. He said she'd left San Amaro and was working as a bartender, but he didn't know where. Julia interrupted her story to ask whether she remembered how Malcolm said he'd heard from her. Then she clarified her question. "Did he say who called whom?"

There was silence for a few moments, then Mona answered slowly, as though a new thought was emerging in her mind. "I think he said he called her, but that doesn't make sense unless she got a new number. But then, how would he have know it. I was still calling her phone once or twice a day, leaving messages until the mailbox was full, and getting no response. I don't know why I didn't think about that then."

"Can you tell me more about Heather? The kind of person she was," Julia asked.

"Heather was fun-loving, smart, funny, a bit of an old hippie, and footloose. Though she didn't talk a lot about her past, it seemed like she moved around whenever the mood hit her. I suppose that's why I believed Malcolm when he said she'd left town. I think she had gotten some money when her mom died, not a fortune or anything, but enough to give her a cushion so she didn't have to work all the time."

"Did she have hobbies or activities she participated in?

"She loved being in the water. She did water aerobics, and sometimes, I'd join her. She also loved just swimming laps. She wasn't enamored of swimming in the sea, though. Said it was something to do with the movie Jaws. I never knew if she was serious or just joking."

Julia waited, hoping there was more.

"One time when we were at the pools, she'd brought one of those water blaster toy guns. You know the ones that are huge, like a bazzoka."

Julia nodded for her to go on.

"It was a Saturday, and the big pool was full of kids. The children of weekend renters, I guess. Anyway, they were making it hard for us to swim, so Heather blasted them with the water gun. They thought it was a game, and she and they had an all-out water battle for about ten minutes, until the kids got bored and decided to get in the hot tub. That was Heather. She got rid of the kids, but with fun, not a fight."

When it was clear Mona had no more stories of her friend, Julia thanked her and said goodbye.

Julia found a phone number on the Colorado Department of Transportation website and silently wished herself luck. After being transferred several times, she finally spoke to a woman in the department's human resources group. As she began to launch into her request, she had the briefest mental picture of Alma calling schools asking about red-haired girls named Heather. But that had paid off. Maybe she'd get lucky too.

She was smiling when she launched into her request. "I'm calling from the police and I'm trying to locate a man who worked for the state government of Colorado in Denver in logistics fifteen years ago. Are you the right person to speak with?" Getting an affirmative answer, she continued.

"I don't have a lot of information about him, but here's what I do know. He is called Dutch. He was in San Amaro, Mexico—that's on the east side of the Baja peninsula—in October of 2010. He is tall, broad-shouldered, blond, and was riding his motorcycle with a group of other men. They were returning to the States after a trip to Cabo. I'm sorry, I don't know anything else about him."

Julia was put on hold. It was a very long wait during which she wondered more than once if she'd been cut off. Finally, the line came alive and a man's voice greeted her.

"Hi, I'm Len. So, you're looking for Dutch, eh?" The voice was gravelly and inflected with interest. "Do you mind me asking what this is about?"

"I'd just like to speak with him about his time in San Amaro in 2010."

"Well, Dutch retired a couple of years ago, but I can get you his cell number. I was on that trip too. Can I help you at all?"

This was better than Julia could have hoped. She got Dutch's phone number and Len also gave her a good description of the night at the Cha-Cha Club. It mostly tallied with the account she'd heard from both Mona and Laurie. She learned the four men had left the club at closing and returned to their hotel. They left San Amaro the next day at about eleven. Julia thanked him and dialed the number he had given her.

"This is Dutch," a mellow voice said after only two rings. Julia introduced herself and explained she was calling to learn more about his visit to San Amaro. She didn't tell him anything else and could understand the uncertainty in his voice as he slowly intoned one word. "Okay."

She led him through the events of that night, hearing the now-familiar story of four men and four women innocently dancing and partying together. The description of the men leaving and returning to their hotel matched what she'd just heard from Len. So far, so good. Time for the harder questions.

"Please tell me about your relationship with Heather Holstaff."

"Who?"

"You may have known her as Red. I believe that's what her friends called her."

"Oh, her," Dutch said. "Well, I wouldn't call it a relationship. We had some dances together and chatted outside the club while we smoked a couple of times. But I didn't even ask for her phone number when the guys and I left. I'm a happily married man. I wasn't looking for anything more than someone to dance with. Honestly, I haven't given her a thought since that night. Now, what is this about?"

"Did you see her again before you left San Amaro?" Julia asked.

There was no response. Julia held her breath. Was he stalling? Had they somehow gotten it all wrong? Was this man involved?

Perhaps he'd followed Malcolm and Heather home and had a clandestine meeting that turned violent with her further into the morning's wee hours. She heard muffled sounds from the phone, but not another word from Dutch.

Her suspicion with on high alert.

Chapter Thirty-Six – Present Day

"Sir, are you still there?" Julia finally said, wondering what he was doing. She could hear muffled sounds but got no response. Then the line went silent. Julia thought their call had been cut off. Then she considered another option.

Dutch had just hung up on her. She had asked him if he'd seen Heather again before he and his buddies left San Amaro. He'd hesitated. Then he'd hung up. The implications exploded into a million conflicting thoughts in her brain.

Julia hit the redial button and held her breath: one ring, two, three. Her mouth went dry. After eight rings it went to voicemail. She hung up. She had the horrible feeling that the case they had felt so confident in was built on sand. She took several deep breaths to calm herself and clear her mind. Julia picked up her phone again.

"Hello, is this Len? It's Detective Sergeant Garcia calling again. I have more questions."

She learned that Len and Dutch had shared a room at their hotel that evening. He verified that Dutch and he had risen at nine the following morning, breakfasted with their riding buddies, and then all readied their bikes for their return trip to Denver. Dutch had been with Len the entire morning.

"Did Dutch return to your hotel room with you after leaving the club?" she asked. Getting an affirmative response, she relaxed slightly. It didn't last.

"Did he go out again that night, after you returned from the club?" She was praying he'd say no. Then they'd be able to rule Dutch out.

"I don't know. He was still dressed when I fell asleep."

She found Ricardo updating the inspector about finding Heather's dance partner's name and getting a phone number for Mona, the birthday party honoree.

"I just spoke with Dutch. Heather's dance partner at the club. He was all friendly and helpful until I asked if he'd seen Heather later in the evening after they all left the club. He hung up on me, and subsequent calls all went to voicemail. Apart from his phone number, all I know is that he's in Denver. His roommate that night couldn't verify if Dutch had left their hotel room that night. So, I think we now have two potential suspects, Malcolm and Dutch."

Julia and Ricardo stood in front of a cream-colored, single-story house with pale green trim, a sky-blue door, and a black-painted wrought iron gate barring access to the small courtyard leading to the door. A derelict fountain in the courtyard's center was crowned with two dolphins playing atop a waterless concrete wave. A lock secured the gate. No one was home.

This area of the Oasis was the oldest and most densely populated. There was a house on almost every lot. The landscaping was more mature than in the newer sections.

The duo noticed movement inside the house next door and knocked on the door. Julia told the woman who answered that they were looking for her neighbor, Malcolm Davenport. The woman introduced herself simply as Kate and told them he'd been gone for a few days, maybe a week.

"It was strange. I was outside watering my trees," she told the police. "He left for water volleyball like he does most days, though that day he drove over. Then, not five minutes later, he sped up here in a cloud of dust, parked his truck there," she said, pointing to a battered twenty-year-old Chevy pickup in the driveway. "He ran into the house, came back out a couple of minutes later with a suitcase, and spun out of here in his car like the devil was on his tail. He didn't say a word. But then, he's not the most friendly person, even on a good day. I haven't seen him since."

Kate confirmed she didn't have any idea where Malcolm was going. They spoke for a few minutes during which Julia learned what little Kate knew of her neighbor. Malcolm was generally quiet, except when he had his poker nights when it could get loud late in the night when his cronies left. Also, he had a routine. House chores and shopping in the mornings, volleyball at midday, brewery in the afternoons, and TV or poker in the evenings.

He's a man who likes his habits. That might be useful. She filled Ricardo in on the parts of the conversation he hadn't understood as they drove away, and finished by adding her heartfelt appreciation for nosy neighbors…as long as they weren't her neighbors.

She'd call Malcolm when they returned to the station.

Three scraggly old gringo dudes sat at the dimly lit bar of an equally scraggly drinking establishment in a dusty back alley in La Paz. YouTube videos of skateboard wipe-outs played on a TV over the bar and vied for the patrons' attention with a soccer game on another TV on the side wall. Malcolm's phone was sitting on the bar beside his glass of beer. It was ringing. It was a San Amaro number and not one he knew. He turned off the ringer and stuffed the phone in his back pocket.

He'd feared this since the moment he saw the poster with Heather's face staring at him. That image haunted him, and not just in his dreams. He had now started seeing her face on people in the street, in stores, on every redhead he saw. He didn't know what to do. *Fight, flight, or freeze*. He was frozen.

There was no one to fight, and he had already fled. He could not get his mind to clear long enough to think through a plan of what to do next. In his clearer moments, he knew the alcohol wasn't helping, but he couldn't bear to face his situation without it.

Now Callum was on his case too. What did he know? Should he go somewhere else? Where? And to do what?

He ordered another beer with a whiskey chaser and gazed unseeing at videos of stupid kids trying to impress their friends with ridiculous skateboard tricks.

He'd figure out what to do later.

Julia left a voice message on Malcolm's cell instructing him to call her as soon as possible. "He's not going to answer or call me back," Julia said in exasperation as she set her phone down. "Do you have any ideas how we can find him, Ricky?"

Ricardo had been working on a laptop while she'd been on the phone and looked up with a quirky smile that made his handsome face even more appealing. "This app might help. What's the phone number?" Ricardo typed in the digits as Julia told him and in seconds, looked up with an even bigger grin. "I found his cell carrier. We should be able to get a warrant compelling his phone's location. If you start preparing that, I'll get Hector's approval."

Detective Inspector Hector Martinez, their direct boss, had an office just a few doors away from their war room. Ricardo updated him, and Hector applauded their idea to track Malcolm's phone.

"Bring me the warrant paperwork when it's prepared, and I'll get it signed."

Chapter Thirty-Seven – Present Day

Ricardo had been on his desk phone since Julia arrived the following morning and got settled in the war room.

"Wow, these telecom folks are amazing!" Ricardo said as he burst into the room. "I have the GPS location of Malcolm's phone. The actual GPS location. He's in a resort community on the north side of La Paz. They even told me he's in the Blue Block. Here, let me show you."

He busied himself on his computer for a second, then turned the laptop to face Julia. It showed the Google Earth aerial view of what looked like a huge complex with houses and condos clustered around a golf course. A red bubble pinned to a larger building—it looked like an apartment block—showed what Julia now knew was the Blue Block.

"So, our person of interest has absconded to La Paz. Do you know the name of that resort complex?" Julia asked. Ricardo provided the name, and she found the number and called. She was on hold for a long time, so Ricardo decided to get a fresh coffee. When he returned. A beaming Julia informed him that someone named Callum Davenport owned a condo in the Blue Block of the resort. "I'm guessing he's a brother."

The pair had to wait for nearly an hour for Inspector Martinez to finish a meeting. As soon as he was free, they filled him in on the latest and asked his recommendation about how to get Malcolm back to San Amaro.

The three discussed the possibility that Malcolm would know what happened to Heather and was possibly her killer. Eventually, the three moved down the hall to the comandante's corner office. Ricardo and Julia let Martinez do all the talking until it came to the details of their investigation.

When the comandante felt he understood the situation well, the sergeants were dismissed while the brass continued their conversation. Over an hour later, Hector joined them in the war room.

"Okay, here's the plan. The Baja Sur police in La Paz will pick Malcolm up and drive him to Mulege, where we will get him. Since it's more than seven hours to get there, I've found a hostel for an overnight stay. La Paz police will let us know when they have collected him."

Ricardo shifted in his chair, giving Julia a raised eyebrow before turning back to face Hector. "When is this going to happen?"

"We can do the handoff today if they collect him before eleven. I'd like you two to pick him up. So, head home, pack a go-bag, then get back here. I'll let you know as soon as I hear."

Callum opened his door to an unexpected knock and was shocked to see two police officers standing at his door. When they asked if he was Malcolm, he said no and called his brother to the door. "What the hell have you done, Malc?" Then, to the police, he asked, "Where are you taking him? Can I bail him out or something?"

In broken English, the taller officer explained they were to take him to Mulege, where officers from the San Amaro police would return him to his home. Again, Callum turned to his brother, his face ashen and angry. "Call me when you can. I'll drive your car to San Amaro and see you there. And you'd better explain to me what's going on."

The drive from San Amaro to Mulege was through varied and beautiful terrain. For the first couple of hours, the cruiser hugged the coastline on Highway Five, which offered Ricardo and Julia gorgeous views of the Sea of Cortez.

The road then turned inland and westward to join Highway One in Chapala. For the next hour, Dr. Suess-like trees, called Boojum, gave the landscape a whimsical appearance with their skinny, twisting stalks crowned by sprigs of delicate red and pink flowers.

They stopped at a restaurant near Guerrero Negro for a late lunch of spicy birria stew and carne asada tacos. Fortified by their delicious meal, they headed south and east, back across the peninsular mountains toward the Sea of Cortez, then south to the small town of Mulege. It was getting dark as they arrived at the State Police station there.

The officers from La Paz arrived shortly after and handed Malcolm over to Julia and Ricardo. They learned that the detainee hadn't said anything during the car ride. But since he didn't speak Spanish and neither of them spoke English well, that wasn't surprising.

Julia explained to their charge that they'd be taking him to San Amaro the following day to answer questions about a death that occurred fifteen years before. Malcolm's face drained of color, though his face remained surprisingly impassive.

This must be his poker face.

Chapter Thirty-Eight – Present Day

Callum was beyond worried about his brother. Neither of them had been in trouble with the police before. At least, as far as he knew. The more he thought about how moody and evasive Malcolm had been since joining him in La Paz, the more concerned he became.

They had been so close for many years. As the miles of the nearly fourteen-hour drive to San Amaro clicked by, his mind drifted back to that time.

Callum had signed on with a commercial fisherman as a deckhand shortly after graduating from high school and was amazed that in his first season, he made what he considered to be a small fortune. The boat on which he crewed was out of Anacortes, Washington, and troll-fished primarily for King Salmon from May through July in Alaska and in the fall, offshore from the mouth of the Columbia River.

When Malcolm graduated, he joined Callum for the Alaska fishing season. By then, Callum had been promoted to the job of fish handler. As a deckhand, he'd shown an innate awareness of proper care of the fish once they were onboard. How they were processed—cleaning, bleeding, filleting, sorting, and storage—greatly impacted the income generated from a catch. A good fish handler was a prize.

During his second year at sea, Callum worked with the fish handler, impressing him with his knife skills. The year Malcolm joined the crew, Callum managed the processing job himself. He'd tried to train his brother in the processes he performed, but Malcolm said it was too finicky for him. He preferred the manual labor and the physical demands of working the lines. Malcolm had never been highly motivated, preferring to be a worker, never a boss.

After his first season of fishing, Callum knew it was what he wanted to spend his life doing. He found that by living a modest lifestyle when on land and supplementing his seasonal fishing work with odd jobs, he was able to save most of his fishing earnings.

At the end of his eighth year of fishing, he had saved enough to buy a well-maintained, medium-sized, used troller. Malcolm had joined him as an employee.

Malcolm never could hold on to money or girlfriends.

The thought brought him back to the present and the recent memory of Malcolm's lie about Neil Diamond CDs and an old girlfriend who'd come back to haunt him. Knowing Malc, his story likely held more than a grain of truth, meaning a woman was involved in whatever was happening. And, knowing his brother, he would bet it had something to do with Malcolm's uncontrollable jealousy.

He recalled Malcolm's first girlfriend back in high school. They got on great for over half of the tenth grade, and then the girl, Ida, got involved in a play. She had after-school rehearsals. Malcolm flipped out that she wasn't available whenever he wanted to do something with her.

One phone call Callum overheard, Malcolm was almost screaming at her, he was so angry. Not surprisingly, she told him to get stuffed. The next day, Malc had been sent home from school for spray painting BITCH on Ida's locker. Unfortunately, it was a repeating pattern in Malcolm's life. A chill snaked up Callum's spine.

How much worse would his reaction be now that he was drinking so heavily?

Callum had hoped to make it to Guerrero Negro before nightfall, but as he neared San Ignacio, he decided to call it a day. He'd been driving more than seven hours, and it was starting to get dark. He found a small hotel on the main square of the tiny town and delicious tacos two doors down.

As he ate, his memory lane took a divergent path. A long-buried memory emerged of the day he took possession of his first troller. The green-eyed monster in his brother had surfaced with him as the target.

Malcolm railed about how lucky Callum was, how everything always went his way, and was easy for him. Callum had been stunned. Surely, his brother had witnessed how hard he'd worked as a deckhand and then a fish handler. He was always working, always saving, even in the off-season while Malcolm partied with friends.

Callum had taken any job he could find and occasionally lived in friends' basements when on land. Malcolm, on the other hand, always had an apartment and a gym membership.

Callum's rebuttal of 'the harder I work, the luckier I get' elicited only a cynical laugh from Malcolm. The memory carried a great sadness as Callum recognized the enormity of the chip Malcolm had on his shoulder.

Envy, jealousy, and an unearned sense of entitlement plagued his younger brother. That couldn't be a happy or healthy lens through which to view the world.

Barring incident, he'd get to San Amaro by one the following afternoon. A deep foreboding permeated his being and haunted his sleep.

What did Malcolm do to get the police involved?

Chapter Thirty-Nine – Present Day

Inspector Martinez had advised Julia and Ricardo not to interview the man until he was back in San Amaro. He wanted all interviews with Malcolm to be recorded and videotaped. Malcolm was the last person seen with Heather. At the very least that made him a person of interest. Given the way the crime had been covered up, literally tossing the woman in a cistern and bricking it over. And the fact he fled to La Paz as soon as the facial reconstruction posters went up led Martinez to believe Malcolm would prove difficult to interview.

On the drive from Mulege to San Amaro, Malcolm tried several approaches to get the police to tell him something, but to no avail. His final attempt was a simple denial. “I don’t know what you think I’ve done, but you’ve got the wrong guy. I haven’t broken any laws. This is harassment. I was just visiting my brother, for Christ’s sake.”

Ricardo’s response was to find a Cumbia station on the radio and turn it up loud. Julia smiled ruefully and shook her head. Her partner’s simple solutions amused and impressed her. He intuitively knew that not engaging was their best option. She wasn’t sure she’d have thought of such an easy way to shut Malcolm up.

Malcolm figured his escorts’ unwillingness to talk with him must mean they were either nothing more than a transport detail or they’d been instructed not to talk to him. The fact they were wearing street clothes, not uniforms, most likely meant they were detectives. His chest felt as though it were wrapped in a very tight steel band. He felt like gulping in great mouthfuls of air, but willed his breath to follow a steady rhythm. He longed for a drink to calm himself.

As the drive dragged on and on, his mind whirled. His thoughts ricocheted from frustration at Heather's infidelity—which Malcolm now believed to be fact—to fears that Callum had been spying on him since his arrival in La Paz and had alerted the police to his whereabouts.

He saw himself as the wronged party in his memories of the night Heather left him. Even though she'd gone out with another man, drinking and dancing all night, he'd been a gentleman and picked her up. She'd been so drunk she'd slipped in the bathroom of the club and caused a fatal injury to herself. And she died on the drive home. All he'd done was to bury her in a crypt. He'd even bricked over the crypt entrance so she wouldn't be exposed to the elements.

And he saw himself as the wronged party sitting in a police cruiser being taken back to San Amaro. He hadn't done anything wrong. He was an upstanding person. He'd never been in trouble with the law, and whatever they thought he'd done, they were wrong.

Then a frightening thought settled in his addled mind. Whatever crime these cops thought he'd committed, they planned to pin it on him.

Callum had been to San Amaro several times when Malcolm had first moved there. But he didn't know how to get to his brother's new place. He didn't know the location of the State Police Station either. He was tired of driving—Malcolm's old SUV was not as comfortable as his Lexus—and hungry when he arrived, so went directly to the Malecon in search of food, a comfortable place to sit and watch the sea, and someone to give him directions to the cop shop.

He found a narrow taqueria with outdoor seating wedged between two nightclubs. It had a perfect view of the fishermen cleaning their catch in San Amaro Bay. The sight took his mind back to his fish-processing days. He was grateful to have worked on decked boats rather than open boats, like the pangas before him. Those fishermen were constantly vulnerable to the elements.

After a delicious lunch of shrimp quesadilla and two carne asada tacos, Callum got directions to the police station and headed there. He had little difficulty finding it. It was located on the main north-south drag, Calle Guadalajara, about halfway between the Malecon and the north edge of town. The tan-colored, two-story building had seen better days. Stucco, damaged by rain, heat, and neglect, had broken in places leaving gray cinderblocks peeking out.

Callum parked in a sandy lot and entered a small foyer with several mismatched chairs and posters of criminals and missing persons. An officer was seated behind a plywood desk. Rightly assuming he was the desk sergeant, he approached and asked in halting Spanish if his brother and his police escorts had arrived yet. The sergeant made a quick call and informed Callum that they were about twenty minutes away and suggested he take a seat.

While he waited, he used the translator app on his phone to ask the desk sergeant if he would be able to see his brother when he arrived. After another short phone call, the sergeant told him someone would talk to him once his brother arrived. Moments later, Inspector Martinez strode into the foyer, introduced himself to Callum, and suggested that they go upstairs to his office. It was clear to

Callum that the inspector spoke about as much English as he spoke Spanish.

Should be an interesting chat.

The Inspector rifled through papers on his desk and pulled out a photograph of an attractive, red-haired woman, asking if Callum knew her. Callum shook his head but his mind was whirling. It wasn't a complete lie. He had never met the woman. But he'd seen her face on Malcolm's Facebook feed. Years ago. This photo was clearly of a facial reconstruction, and he knew his brother had a soft spot for redheads. An icy pit filled the space normally occupied by his stomach.

What had Malcolm done?

Chapter Forty – Present Day

Malcolm had been placed in Interview Room One upon his arrival at the station. Once Julia and Ricardo had readied the camera and microphones from that room to connect with Ricardo's desk computer, Inspector Martinez brought Callum in to speak with his brother. The three officers gathered around Ricardo's desk to listen to their conversation using the voice translation software to hear the brothers' exchange in Spanish.

"What the hell, Malc? Tell me what's going on." Callum looked frantic and spoke with quiet urgency.

Malcolm tipped his head up and to the right and used his eyes to point to the camera mounted at the junction of wall and ceiling, then moved his gaze to the recording equipment on the table. A small red light indicated it was recording. Callum nodded, acknowledging that whatever Malcolm said next was for the benefit of the listeners, not him.

"I think it's about a woman who lived with me years ago. I gather she died shortly after she moved out. Last I heard, she was a bartender somewhere. I thought she'd gone back to Mulege to her previous boyfriend, but maybe she stayed here. I haven't seen her since she packed up her car and left my place. It's got to be fifteen years ago."

Callum asked if Malcolm wanted him to hire a lawyer, to which his brother said with mad bravado that he didn't need one. It frightened Callum, causing him, for the first time, to question his brother's grip on reality. Now, however, was not the time to probe further. The police advised him to leave. So, after getting directions to Malcolm's home, he left the station. He was more worried than he'd been since the police arrived at his door.

Before they headed to the interview room, Martinez told Ricardo and Julia about Luis's desire to become a detective constable. Julia smiled happily at the news. "I've asked him to stand in for this interview. I know he won't understand everything, but it will still be beneficial for him. I'll have him stand by the door. It might put a bit more pressure on our suspect, as well."

Once the three police officers joined Malcolm in the interview room and Luis had taken up his guard position, Julia and Inspector Martinez started the interview. Ricardo, still listening and watching at his desk, settled in. They said their names for the recording and had Malcolm do the same. They had decided to start softly, to get a baseline of how he spoke, sat, and moved while answering regular questions. So, Julia's first question simply aimed to get him talking. "How long have you lived in San Amaro, Mr. Davenport?"

From there, the questions covered easily verifiable things like how long he'd lived in each of his homes, what vehicles he owned, and what he did for recreation, and what he'd done for work before he retired. Next, the questions shifted to when he'd left San Amaro to visit his brother, whether or not he lived alone, had been married, or had a current girlfriend. So far, he appeared to be telling the truth. They would verify his answers to be sure. As he answered, Julia could see the man's shoulders drop an inch or two. He was starting to relax. Time to shift the questioning.

"Tell me about Heather Holstaff." Julia's tone was conversational. Ricardo, earphones in place, sat up in his chair. Time to pay very close attention to the suspect's demeanor and body language. He, too, had noticed Malcolm relax over the past couple of minutes and was impressed anew at Julia's ability to know just the right time to turn up the heat and by how many degrees.

Malcolm started at the beginning. He'd met Heather in Mulege where she was bartending at the only hotel on the main square. He was there for a week doing some Marlin fishing. He and Heather had a connection. He nicknamed her Red the second night he was at the bar.

On his third day there, Red told him she was shacked up with a guy, but that she was looking to make a move. They started flirting. His last night there, she spent the night with him, and when he left, she told him not to be surprised if she showed up on his doorstep. Two weeks later, she did.

He explained they lived together for almost two years, but that they maintained a pretty casual relationship. Heather did her thing, and he did his. When asked what those things were he told them that in addition to water aerobics, Heather had been a regular at pickleball, enjoyed golf, and was part of a walking group.

Because of a previous case, Julia knew many people who regularly played pickleball at the Oasis. She made a note to remind herself to check with them to verify Malcolm's story, if necessary.

"What were the circumstances around her leaving your house?" Julia had been tempted to say 'leaving you', but the gloves weren't that far off yet.

Malcolm said a momentary thank you to his fifteen-year-ago self for writing his story about Heather's departure. He told it now with ease.

The three police officers witnessing his interview were surprised at how his demeanor remained constant while he answered. They had all expected him to show some sign of tension or deception.

The man didn't break eye contact while blinking naturally—no looking up and to the right. He didn't fidget or freeze. His skin tone didn't change—no flushing or blanching—and no sweating. Even his vocal tone, speed, and phrasing remained the same as with the baseline questions. Julia caught her mind focusing on these things rather than his words and was grateful it was being recorded. She would read the transcript later to ensure she hadn't missed anything important.

When asked when Heather's departure occurred, Malcolm became vague—about fifteen years ago, he'd said. Julia tried to pin him down by asking in which month she'd left. That question appeared to fluster him. His face flushed and Julia noticed his eyes gaze unseeingly to the right for a moment, then snap straight ahead as if he'd realized what he was doing.

"It was May, likely mid-month," Malcolm said calmly, though his voice cracked slightly. *Well, that was a lie*, Julia thought. Inspector Martinez rattled off something in Spanish, to which Julia nodded. They were ready to turn the screws.

"The truth, Mr. Davenport, is that Heather went missing on October ninth or tenth. And, since you've just lied to us about that, I'm going to assume that everything you've told us about her has been lies. Would you like to revise your statement before we continue?"

Malcolm had not previously had a run-in with Mexican police. He'd been working under the assumption that they were mostly an untrained bunch of ruffians. He'd heard they were grossly underpaid and figured they'd only attract people who couldn't find a better job. He was rapidly beginning to reevaluate those assumptions. This woman seemed well-trained and highly educated. Perhaps he *should* have Callum find him a lawyer.

"Mr. Davenport, we're going to give you some time to think. Perhaps your memory of events surrounding Heather's departure will improve," Julia said. The inspector had Luis take Malcolm to the cells at the back of the station.

They'd speak with him again in a few hours. Or maybe tomorrow.

Chapter Forty-One – Present Day

As Julia parked La Chica beside an aging SUV in front of Malcolm's house, she noticed his nosy neighbor was again watering her trees and wondered if that daily activity was simply to cover her surveillance. She acknowledged the woman's presence with a small wave and a 'Hi Kate' as she and Ricardo approached the sky-blue door.

Callum answered, looking behind the police, no doubt hoping to see his brother. His face fell when he realized Malcolm wasn't with them. Julia explained they needed to ask Callum some more questions. They were invited into the small but cozy living room with a kitchen at the opposite end of the room. The walls, a warm cream color, obviously painted over wallpaper, provided a neutral background for the wild mishmash of colors, patterns, and styles of the room's furniture. The effect was garish.

Ricardo and Julia sat together on a vivid plaid couch in navy blue, blood red, and pale yellow. Callum sat opposite on a worn and fraying brown corduroy recliner. Beads of sweat dotted his forehead and he held his body in a rigid posture Julia was sure would leave him with aching shoulders. Julia began by getting background on Malcolm. Where had they lived in their youth? *Bellingham, Washington.* What work had Malcolm done? *Commercial fishing.* Did they have other siblings? *No.* Were he and Malcolm close?

Reasonably. How had Malcolm ended up in San Felipe? *Not sure.* Had Malcolm ever been married? *No.*

When asked to describe their lives growing up, Callum painted a picture of a hard-working, lower-middle-class family. Their father was a welder. Their mother had stayed home until the early 1960s when Malcolm, the youngest, was old enough to attend kindergarten. Then she'd returned to work as a supermarket cashier. Their parents were strict, and right and wrong were clearly defined with praise and punishment both liberally provided.

Callum was forthcoming, answering her questions promptly and easily, and providing the information Julia requested with no hesitation. Upon learning Malcolm had never married or been in any long-term relationships, Julia began to probe deeper. "Why do you think he never had more permanent relationships?"

This question seemed to stump the brother. He took several moments before answering. Julia suspected he was pondering the question. Callum, however, knew the reason but was hesitant to share it with the police. If only he knew more about what had happened. If only he knew for a fact that Malcolm hadn't done anything to that woman.

Julia quickly realized the man was preparing to fabricate an answer and stopped him before he could. "Mr. Davenport, lying to the police is a crime. And it could possibly harm your brother's defense if he is charged with a crime against his old girlfriend."

Callum's words, when he finally spoke, were completely true, but perhaps not the complete truth. It was the best he could do. He wasn't about to lie to these people and put himself in danger, but also, he didn't want to give them information that could harm his brother.

"Malcolm always wants things to be easy. When something isn't easy, he generally walks away. Relationships are usually easy for the first year or two, but then things can start chafing. Things you were willing to overlook start to become problems, and arguments occur. If that happened with the woman, Heather, I could see Malcolm withdrawing emotionally. Not many women are willing to stick around when that happens."

Julia agreed with his evaluation that women want emotional connection, while also realizing his answer was very general. "Can you give me an example of what might cause this chaffing, specifically for Malcolm?"

Damn, Callum thought, *this woman doesn't let anything slip past her.*

Ricardo leaned over and spoke quietly to Julia. Yes, she'd noticed it too. Callum visibly tensed even more with the last question. They were getting close to something important.

Malcolm had only been in the cell for a few hours, but already he was getting antsy. *How did people survive, mentally, when stuck in a cell for years?* Initially, he'd thought it might be best to tell them about Heather's fall in the women's bathroom of the Cha-Cha Club. From what he'd read on Google, he figured that's what killed her.

He berated himself for being too drunk to think through his actions that night. If he'd called the police the moment he realized she was dead, he'd have been fine. But that's not what he did. He'd covered the whole thing up. He'd put her body into an abandoned cistern. Then he'd bricked over the top of the damned thing. The cops would see his actions as those of a killer. They'd never believe him now, even though he was innocent.

The longer he was in the cell, the more his mind shifted to creating an alibi. He tried to remember everything he'd done that night. He'd kicked his poker buddies out early. The cops could verify that. Then he had driven downtown, bought a six-pack, which they didn't need to know about, and parked his truck on the street just below the Cha-Cha Club. As he remembered watching the door to the club and seeing Red and the big blond dude, Malcolm's anger at her betrayal flared again.

Why did the women in his life always treat him so badly? Was no one faithful anymore? Then, just a flicker of a thought ruined his righteous anger. *You're the common denominator in all those bad relationships.*

But he couldn't stay with that idea, had never been able to look at his part in the ruination of all his romantic partnerships. As always, he took refuge from self-reflection in his own righteousness. He was the wronged party. It was as simple as that.

With his self-doubt carefully pushed aside yet again, Malcolm turned his mind fully to fine-tuning his story before the next interrogation.

Chapter Forty-Two – Present Day

"Can you give me an example of what might cause this relationship chaffing you mentioned, specifically for Malcolm?" Julia's question to Callum hung in the air. Neither she nor Ricardo moved. The question had hit a nerve. Callum's jaw tensed, 1qq and the vein in his temple became pronounced.

Callum had tried to skirt the truth of his brother's myriad failed relationships. But now he feared he was trapped. He wasn't cut out for lying—wasn't good at it. It might be time Malcolm faced the truth about his jealousy, but Callum didn't want to be the catalyst for that introspection. Could he give the police some information, but none that might be the key to convicting Malc of something heinous?

Callum's emotions played out on his face, and still Julia and Ricardo waited. Finally, the man's shoulders relaxed, and his face turned to stone. But after another minute, he still had not spoken.

"Is your brother the jealous type, Mr. Davenport? Does he have a temper? Is he physically violent with women? What are you afraid of telling us?"

"Yes, alright, he can be jealous," Callum said angrily. "But that doesn't mean he'd do anything physical. He just gets frustrated when things don't go as he'd hoped." Callum's words were spoken with staccato precision. He was angry. Angry at Julia, she suspected, because she'd made him admit something he'd hoped to keep hidden. Something that might put his brother in jeopardy. She needed to shift the conversation temporarily to keep him from clamming up.

"I noticed an old pickup truck parked by the side of the house. Is that your brother's?" Julia asked. When Callum nodded, she continued in that vein. "Do you have any problem with my partner having a look inside Malcolm's vehicles?" After a moment's hesitation, he agreed, and Ricardo went to search them, though for what he wasn't sure. It had been a very long time since Heather could have been in either vehicle.

"Have you visited your brother here in San Amaro previously?" Julia asked.

Callum told her he'd been there a couple of times when Malcolm first moved to Mexico. "I didn't have a place in La Paz then, and I was interested in seeing what living in Mexico was like. I could see how much he loved it here, and it got me thinking about it myself. I wanted someplace I could fly to and from. San Amaro is great, but the airport is too small for today's passenger planes."

Julia asked if he'd met any of Malcolm's girlfriends. Had he met Heather? Callum explained that he'd never even heard of Heather and concluded that he thought theirs must have been a casual relationship. He was reinforcing the remark Malcolm made before his interrogation.

"Oh, so you have known some of his previous partners?" Julia asked, taking advantage of the opening.

Callum admitted he'd only met a couple of the women his brother had dated since they quit fishing together, and those had been almost twenty years ago. Still, Julia persisted, and he eventually shared the names of two women Malcolm had dated in Bellingham whom he'd met while the brothers both still lived there.

"Thank you for your time, Mr. Davenport. We may need to speak with you again. Please let us know if you're planning on leaving before our investigation is over." She left a business card on a small table near the door.

When Ricardo returned from the vehicle search, the pair departed. Julia guessed Ricardo had found something in his search because he was as fidgety as a child with ADHD forced to sit through a Sunday sermon. "Bien, vaciar el costal." *Okay, empty the sack,* she said, using an expression equivalent to 'spill the beans'.

Ricardo held up two small evidence bags. In one, Julia could see something tiny, gold, and very fine. The other held what looked like a pebble. He explained that Malcolm's truck was filthy inside and speculated it likely hadn't been cleaned in the last fifteen years. The passenger footwell had a floormat that was almost welded to the floorboards with grime, but when he'd managed to pull it up, Ricardo had found an earring back with about an inch of thin gold chain attached.

Typical of her partner, Julia knew he'd save the more important find for last. As he held up the second evidence bag, he explained that in the carpet under the floormat, amid many real pebbles, he'd found a pea-sized piece of tooth.

If it was the missing piece of the broken tooth in the skull, this might be the first piece of evidence directly linking Malcolm to Heather's death.

At the station, Julia took the evidence bags to Vicente and asked if he could make them a priority. While she was still in the forensic lab, he opened the bag containing the earring back with its attached tiny gold chain. On his computer, he opened one of the photos Julia had gotten from Laurie Graham and enlarged it on the screen. It was taken in the Cha-Cha Club the night of Mona Richardson's birthday party and showed Heather and a blond man at a drink-strewn table.

Vicente continued to enlarge the photo until it was almost blurry and focused the viewing area on Heather's face. Her long red hair was draped over one shoulder, exposing the left side of her face and ear. Vicente pointed to the woman's earring. It appeared as though a fine gold chain was looped through her piercing, the same gold chain in the evidence bag. And a tiny glint, where something reflected the flash, could just be seen through her hair on her shoulder.

Julia realized Heather had worn those earrings the night of the party, the last time any of her friends had seen her. Her pulse quickened with excitement. "Please let me know if you find anything on this and see if the piece of tooth fits the broken molar in the skull."

Next, Julia called Alma, who was back in Mexico City after visiting San Amaro the previous week. She gave her the names of the two women she'd received from Callum, and informed her that twentyish years ago they'd both lived in Bellingham, Washington. It was a long shot, but every lead needed to be checked, and Alma was always happy to do research. Her English skills were close to Julia's, making her better suited to the job than any of the constables in San Amaro.

When they'd returned to the station, Ricardo left in a hurry, mumbling something about an appointment. Julia used the quiet time to update their whiteboards with the latest information as she impatiently awaited news from Vicente.

Chapter Forty-Three – Present Day

Malcolm had been stuck in a cell for almost twenty-four hours and his mind had been on a rollercoaster ride, soaring up to heights of self-righteousness only to plummet into despair at his heinous acts. So too had his ideas on how to respond to the police. Should he come clean and face the consequences of his actions or maintain the story he'd concocted all those years before?

Malcolm's thoughts always bounced back to his self-righteous delusions. She wronged him, was disloyal, and unfaithful. The whole mess was her fault.

When the constable who had guarded the door during his previous interview—he refused to think of it as interrogation—came to retrieve him from the cell, his thoughts were in the 'keep to the original story' vein. Consequently, he walked to the interview room with his head held high and his posture erect and confident. At that moment, he believed he was in the clear. All he'd done was bury an already dead body, albeit not in a proper grave.

The initial process was the same as his previous interview, with two police officers across the table and the young constable guarding the door. The female officer again took the lead, though he could tell the older man was her superior by the deferential tone she took when speaking with him. But his English was almost as bad as Malcolm's Spanish.

Malcolm sat back, looking at the hazel-eyed man before him, and waited for the questions, comfortable in his delusion that he had nothing to worry about.

Before entering the interview room, Julia had spoken with Vicente and learned two things that she'd shared with Ricardo and the inspector. Their consensus was to come at the suspect hard with their new information. The evidence against Malcolm was all circumstantial and might not stand up in court. So, their best case would be to get a confession.

Julia's shoulders throbbed, and her clenched jaw caused a headache. She took a moment to relax her body and calm her mind before commencing.

Solving a fifteen-year-old murder required different investigative skills and relied heavily on forensics. They were gaining confidence that Malcolm was their murderer. Now it was up to her to make this man believe they had sufficient evidence to prove that beyond a reasonable doubt.

Luis had not had the opportunity to watch many interrogations. He was, therefore, very grateful to Inspector Martinez for getting him released from his assignment to observe this one. He had worked with Julia on a couple of other cases and had been present at a few interviews in people's homes or places of work, but this was his first time in a murder interrogation at the station. He recognized immediately the added gravitas that environment imparted.

The room put Malcolm in a foul mood. And remembering his night in the cell firmly entrenched him in his self-righteousness. He would wholeheartedly defend his version of the events of Heather's departure. He didn't know it yet, but his bluster was in for a knock-down, drag-out fight.

"Are you finally ready to tell us the truth about what happened to Heather Holstaff, Mr. Davenport?" Julia asked in a neutral tone. She was prepared for a belligerent reply but had no intention of starting in a defensive position.

"I already told you everything I know about her. Yeah, I got the timing wrong, but it was over fifteen years ago. Do you remember exactly when everything occurred fifteen years ago? It's not humanly possible," Malcolm replied, with thinly veiled aggression.

"We're not here to talk about me. Tell us again about Heather's departure in as much detail as possible. And this time, no lies." The firmness in Julia's voice left no doubt that the gloves were off.

For the next two hours, Julia had Malcolm retell the story several times. She hadn't yet let him know they had new evidence. After his fourth time recounting the time when Heather left, Julia and the inspector left him to brood with Luis to keep him company. Ricardo left his desk and joined them as they ascended the stairs to the war room.

"It's like he's reading from a script," Ricardo said when they were all seated. "His story hasn't changed at all." They'd all noticed. Their suspect was lying. No one described past events the same way with every telling. Yet that is exactly what Malcolm had repeatedly done. He'd changed the wording slightly each time, but the events were told in the same order, using the same cadence, with no added or missing information. They strongly suspected his story was just that, a story.

They decided to leave him in the interview room for an hour and then hit him with their new evidence.

Chapter Forty-Four – Present Day

Ricardo had been exploring a line of inquiry he hadn't yet shared with Julia or the inspector. He knew the Cha-Cha Club had been shuttered thirteen years ago, leaving the building abandoned.

While Julia was talking with Vicente, Ricado had finally reached the building owner's representative and had been granted an opportunity to get inside and look around if he could meet there within the hour. He informed Julia and Martinez, and they agreed to put Malcolm back in his cell while Ricardo investigated. Martinez voiced his concern that it was likely a very long shot, but added it couldn't hurt to check it out.

The mid-November day was warm, with temperatures in the mid-eighties, but as often happens in November, the winds were unrelenting. Seagulls soared around fishing pangas in the bay and appeared to be playing in the thermals rising from the sea.

Andrés Alvarez, their nurse-cum-forensic technician, was unavailable, so Ricardo asked Vicente to join him to gather any evidence they might find. A man, standing on the catwalk leading to the abandoned dance club, awaited their arrival as the squad car parked. He was unsuccessfully trying to keep his comb-over covering a shiny bald spot. Greasy tufts of graying hair danced above his head as the wind won. Introductions were made, and the man opened the main door, saying he'd wait outside as they did whatever they came to do.

Approaching the club, Ricardo noticed the once-black stairs and catwalk were now rust-ravaged. The building itself was in no better shape. The outer walls were sooty-gray, and damage from wind, sand, and storms had all but erased the name painted there.

The inside of the place looked even sadder than the exterior. The mirrored-glass panels behind the bar were cracked and broken with shards lying on the bar and floor like jagged pools of water reflecting the weak light from their flashlights. A few broken chairs and trash littered the cavernous room, providing material against which myriad spiders had built webs. The building's windows had been painted black, though now the paint was scratched and worn off in places. The space felt cave-like.

The pair picked their way through the rubble and cobwebs looking for clues. Vicente headed to the back of the building. Having only been in San Amaro for a few years, he had not been a club patron and didn't know what was back there. He soon discovered there was an office and bathrooms. He did a thorough search through the office and men's room. He figured Heather had likely not been in either, but needed to be systematic.

The door to the women's bathroom was hanging from one remaining hinge. All but one of the toilets had been removed, leaving gaping holes in the floor. The room held the fetid stench of decay. Across from what remained of the stalls was a long counter that had previously held four sinks. The Arborite covering was pitted and scarred with bits broken here and there.

Vicente's flashlight beam stopped when it illuminated the counter's corner closest to the door. When asked later how he'd noticed it, he couldn't say, except that he felt drawn to investigate it. Perhaps it was because of a large chunk of broken Arborite hanging off one edge. Whatever it was, he moved closer and focused his beam on the spot. His closer inspection, however, didn't reveal anything unusual.

Next, he searched the underside of the counter. He called out to Ricardo, who entered the room to see Vicente kneeling, shining his flashlight under the counter. "Can you shine your light under here, too, please?"

With both flashlights illuminating the spot, Vicente spied a dark stain on the plywood along the edge where the countertop was broken as though something had been spilled and had run over the edge. Ricardo took several photos on his phone of the area, then fetched Vicente's evidence-gathering case from the main door where he'd left it.

The forensic specialist scraped a bit of the dark area, put a drop of liquid on the scrapings, then placed a small strip of paper against it. The paper turned greenish-blue.

"It's human blood," Vicente said, excitedly. "I'll get a sample. Maybe it's the victim's."

The two men continued to search the rest of the room but found nothing more that seemed relevant to their case. After an hour in the dusty, smelly black cavern, they emerged, blinking in the sunlight, and went in search of the owner. They found him drinking a Coke on a red plastic chair outside a cantina across the Malecon from the derelict club. Though they didn't know it, he was sitting just feet from where Malcolm had sat watching the club all those years ago.

Ricardo quickly thanked the man for giving them access to the building. Before jumping into the squad car, he asked for the names and numbers of both the cleaner and the bartender who worked the night of Mona's party, giving the man the date in question. The man was not confident he could provide them, but committed to seeing if the owner had that information.

Ricardo and Vicente could hardly wait to get back to the lab to see if the blood was relevant...putting them one step closer to charging the killer.

Chapter Forty-Five – Present Day

Bibliotheca Nacional de México, established in 1833, was chartered by Benito Juárez to preserve Mexican literary heritage. Like the United States Library of Congress, it is the legal depository of all books, journals, and newspapers published in Mexico. Its current home is within the campus of the University of Mexico, in Mexico City.

Alma had a spare hour at the beginning of the day before the library was open to the public. She began the search for the whereabouts of Malcolm's two ex-girlfriends. Given their presence in Bellingham, Washington, decades ago, she searched for the first woman's name and Bellingham, WA.

Wanda Murtaugh, realtor, was the first entry. With a quick phone call, she learned the woman had retired from the real estate brokerage where she'd worked for more than thirty years. The other piece of information garnered from the firm's receptionist was that Wanda still had the same cell number as listed on the internet. One down, one to go.

Googling Brenda Godfrey, Bellingham, WA, did not produce any useful results. Next, Alma tried LinkedIn and Facebook but struck out again, as there were hundreds of them. None, however, with Bellingham in their profile.

The National Library of Mexico was a premier research facility, with subscriptions to myriad specialized databases. She'd try them next.

Within an hour, Alma had a short list of five Brenda Godfrys who could have been in or near Bellingham during the period her cousin had provided based on Callum's information. All her findings were quickly emailed to Julia.

Julia was hard at work in the war room updating the whiteboards when her laptop pinged that she'd received an email. She started with the easiest girlfriend first.

Wanda Murtaugh answered the phone with a bright, chirpy hello. Once Julia told the woman the purpose of her call, saying only that Malcolm was a possible suspect in a case, the chirpiness left her voice. Yes, she'd dated Malcolm for a couple of years back in the nineties. Yes, they'd lived together for most of that time. "What else do you need to know?" the woman asked curtly.

"What ended the relationship?"

"I realized what a jerk he really was," Wanda said flatly.

"Can you be more specific? What made him a jerk?"

"He had entitlement issues. It seemed like he felt I should be available any time he wanted to see me. It had started almost sweetly, as he expressed his disappointment at not being able to, for example, *take you to dinner tonight because you already have plans with your gal pals*. From there, it advanced.

"When we did go out socially together, he never let me out of his sight. It seemed, well…sweet and caring, initially, but then it became suffocating. If I talked to anyone other than him, he'd grill me on everything said, and if it was a man I'd spoken with, why I 'stood so close' to him. You know things like that. I grew to hate it."

"Anything else I should know about him?

"He was needy, jealous, and extremely possessive. He never said he wanted our relationship to be exclusive, but it was clear he felt like he owned me. I wouldn't put up with that."

It was clear to Julia that the picture she was painting was similar to the one she'd gotten from Callum's depiction.

"Was Malcolm ever physically abusive with you?"

The woman's silence created an eerie presage to her admission. "This is embarrassing to talk about. I've never, ever thought of myself as a victim," she said emphatically. "I used to think that battered women must be weak, but when I found myself at the end of his fist when I told him I was going to a party without him, I realized how easily it could happen. I left him then and there, of course, but still I have to live with knowing I allowed myself to be in a relationship with a bully."

Wanda then balanced her depiction of Malcolm, saying he could be very charismatic, and initially, his attentiveness was flattering. Julia knew victims of violence often justified how they ended up in the situation. Julia thanked the woman and let her get back to her day.

Next, Julia began phoning the Brenda Godfreys whom Alma had found. On the third call, she found the woman she sought. Brenda's description of her relationship with Malcolm was very similar to that of Wanda's. Malcolm had been the perfect boyfriend initially. Then it turned into a possessiveness that verged on stalking. The relationship ended just before the two-year mark. When asked about the precipitating event, Wanda refused to talk about it.

"Was he physically aggressive toward you, Ms. Godrey? Is that why you don't want to discuss it?"

"It was so long ago, and it's something I don't like to talk about."

"I can imagine. I am sorry to have to ask, but I'm trying to get justice for a woman who may have died at his hands. Will you help me?"

After a long silence, Brenda responded. "Yes, he hit me when I told him I wouldn't put up with his jealousy. He told me it was because I was untrustworthy and punched me in the stomach."

Julia absorbed this information. Malcolm's character was becoming clearer. Or perhaps she was more clearly understanding the implications of Callum's description of his brother. She thanked Brenda for her honesty before saying goodbye.

Julia flipped through her notebook for her notes on Callum's interview. He'd said Malcolm liked things to be easy. The other side of that coin was the implication that he didn't handle difficulty well. Callum had also said his brother got frustrated when things didn't go the way he wanted and that he could be jealous.

When she added Callum's remarks with Wanda's admission that he'd punched her when she wanted to do something without him, Julia realized Malcolm had never grown out of the spoiled child phase. Malcolm had also been described as having a sense of entitlement.

Julia recalled a class at the police academy where they'd been taught about different personality disorders and mental illnesses. She navigated on her laptop and found the definition of entitlement. *An expectation of special treatment coupled with a lack of empathy usually resulting in a lack of gratitude and a disregard for boundaries and rules.*

It was part of the narcissistic personality disorder. And that would inform her next interrogation of Malcolm Davenport.

Chapter Forty-Six – Present Day

Vicente's first actions were to extract a clean blood sample from the scraping he'd taken from the now-defunct Cha-Cha Club. There hadn't been any viable marrow in Heather Holstaff's bones to obtain a blood sample, so Vicente next tried her teeth. Because of the durability of teeth and the hardness of their enamel coating, they stayed firmly implanted in the jawbone after death, sometimes preserving precious blood cells.

Though he'd been surprisingly sad to do it, Vicente had already dismantled the facial reconstruction to verify the tooth fragment from Malcolm's truck was from Heather. He had been so proud of the work he'd begun and the final result achieved by Araceli, it had felt like an act of violence destroying it. Now, however, he was glad to have access to the whole dentition.

The first two teeth he extracted, both bottom left molars, provided no blood-bearing pulp. His third attempt, a right-side molar, had sufficient pulp to potentially harbor DNA. He'd never personally performed this process, but after reviewing his notes from a demonstration he'd attended and some online reading, he began.

The extracted tooth was cleaned to remove any contaminants that may have remained after the initial cleaning the entire skeleton had undergone. Next, the inner pulp was accessed by sectioning the tooth with a small rotary saw. Since the pulp was calcified, he'd had to scrap it out with a scalpel. With that done, the sample was ready to send to a lab capable of DNA extraction. Fortunately, there was one in San Amaro.

Vicente gathered his samples—the blood scraped from the underside of the bathroom counter and the tooth pulp—and drove them to the one lab in town with the array of specialized equipment and chemicals necessary for DNA testing. Knowing the existence of such resources was necessary for someone in his field. Over time he'd met Ivan, the lab tech with the required DNA training.

Vicente had already phoned the man to alert him to the urgent analysis required. He reminded the lab tech again, in person, that the case of the woman in the cistern might be solved by his results. Even after stressing the critical time element of the findings, he was informed he would get the report in four days.

"Four days! Damn it. We can't hold him for four days unless he's charged, and we don't have enough evidence to get an arrest warrant." Martinez balled his fists, but almost as quickly unclenched them.

Ricardo was the first to speak. "How do we keep him from taking off again?"

Julia chimed in too. "Ricardo's right, sir. He's a flight risk. Can we place him under house arrest with an officer posted outside his house?"

"I'll talk with the commandante and see if he'll authorize it. Keep looking for more evidence."

The commandante agreed to spare the manpower to watch the house. Two officers on six-hour shifts would used a marked police car and sit outside of Malcolm's home. The back door was actually on the side of the house rather than the back giving the constables the ability to park at the front left corner of the house and have a view of both doors.

Julia and Ricardo escorted the man home, where they confiscated his passport. They left him with the admonishments that he would be under twenty-four hour police watch and that the military checkpoints on the roads in and out of San Amaro would not allow him to leave town should he manage to sneak out a window.

They gave him no additional information or warnings, leaving Malcolm feeling cocky and confident they didn't have any evidence to link him to Heather's death. He didn't like the copy car sitting outside his house, but he reframed its presence to mean he was being given police protection.

"Hey, brother, I'm home!" Malcolm called out since Callum had not come into the living area when Malcolm arrived with the police.

Callum emerged from the spare room he was currently calling home. His face was serious, stressed. He said nothing, simply gave Malcolm a top-to-bottom look, and nodded.

"That's hardly the welcome for a man released from prison," Malcolm said half-seriously.

"I heard the police take your passport and tell you that you can't leave town. There's also a police cruiser sitting outside. I'd call that a temporary reprieve, nothing more," Callum grumbled.

"Look, they obviously don't have any evidence tying me to that skeleton. I ain't done nothing wrong, Cal. Stop worrying. Hey, it's only eleven-thirty. We can make it to water volleyball. Are you interested? It's fun!"

Callum declined. He wasn't convinced by his brother's claim the police had nothing on him. They wouldn't have hunted him down in La Paz and sent him back to San Amaro with a police escort on a whim. He was deeply worried about Malcolm and convinced he needed to hire a lawyer for him. But so far, Malcolm was adamant he didn't need one, which made Callum even more concerned.

Callum was beginning to question his brother's mental stability.

Chapter Forty-Seven – Present Day

Julia, Ricardo, and Martinez faced a few days of waiting for the DNA results and spent the remainder of the first day re-evaluating all the evidence they had. Plans were made about how to proceed—one if the DNA matched Heather's and one if it didn't.

Ricardo occupied his time trying to locate the cleaner and bartender from the Cha-Cha Club. He was not overly optimistic that the numbers he'd received from the building owner were still working, and he quickly discovered the bartender's number wasn't.

He had a little bit better luck with the number for the cleaner. A man answered the call and explained that this was his home phone and that his ex-girlfriend, Paola, the cleaner, no longer lived with him. The last time he'd seen her, she was working with Baja Maids, *Criadas de Baja* in Spanish. After contacting the manager of the maid service, he learned that Paola still worked there and provided Ricardo with her cell number.

"Is this Paola?"

"Yes."

I am Detective Sergeant Hernandez. I have a couple of questions about when you were a cleaner at the Cha-Cha Club."

Armed with the information that Malcolm was jealous, physical when angry, and had a sense of entitlement, Julia learning more about these characteristics. She needed to find specific triggers she could use in the next interrogation of their prime suspect.

As Julia made this note to herself during their meeting, she flipped through her notebook to verify that no tasks were outstanding. As she expected, there was only one. Speak with Dutch about his post-Cha-Cha Club activities.

Her perusal also brought something else to the forefront of her mind. She noted that the same phrase appeared in her notes from two separate interviews…*poker nights at Malcolm's*. Mona mentioned that the night of her birthday, Heather had been surprised that Malcolm picked her up because she thought he'd still be playing poker. And Malcolm's nosy neighbor said his poker nights were noisy.

She wanted to find some of those poker buddies and perhaps get lucky enough to find someone who'd been at his poker game the night of Mona's party fifteen years ago. She mentioned her idea to Ricardo, and they agreed it was an excellent place to dig deeper to learn more about the man they considered to be a viable candidate for the role of murderer.

Ricardo was driving La Chica so Julia could make a call. She dialed the number and listened to it ring. Then a woman's voice answered with a simple hello.

"Hi, I'm looking for Dutch. This is his number, isn't it?" Ricardo heard Julia say.

"Dutch, you say? As far as I know, this phone belongs to Walter Bakker." Bewilderment tinged the woman's words.

Julia introduced herself as a police officer and verified she had the right person by providing Dutch's physical description to the woman and getting an affirmative reply. Then she asked to speak with Mr. Bakker.

The woman explained that she was an ICU nurse at Saint Joseph Hospital and that Mr. Bakker had been in a serious car accident. He'd been rear-ended at a traffic light and pushed into the intersection, where another car driving at speed broad-sided his car on the driver's side. He was in a coma. The date of the accident aligned with when Julia and Dutch had been talking.

Maybe he hadn't hung up on her. Was her call a contributing factor in his accident?

After thanking the nurse and promising to call back in a day or two, she shifted her thinking to their upcoming visit to Kate, the nosy neighbor. She mentioned to Ricardo that Malcolm could be home and see them next door. Their discussion ended with the decision that his awareness of their visit might be a good thing. At least he'd know they were still investigating and getting background on him.

For a change, Kate was not watering her trees when they parked at her house. They were invited in, and once they were seated, Julia explained they were interested in speaking with any of Malcolm's poker buddies. Kate initially demurred, saying she really didn't pay much attention to what went on next door. Julia had to clamp her teeth together to keep her lips from twitching and wondered if the woman had any idea how blatant her snooping was.

After some artful prodding from Julia, however, she admitted to having recognized a couple of the men who attended regularly. Unfortunately, she didn't know any of the men's names but provided a description of two fellows she said attended every time and the make and model of the vehicles they drove. She explained the latter by saying she and her husband had owned a car dealership in the States. She knew her cars.

Ricardo and Julia were about to leave when she added that one of the two—the one who drove a Black Ford F150 XLS with a 49er's bumper sticker—was also a regular at water volleyball. She'd seen him several times when she went over to swim. Julia checked the time and realized that the daily game was due to start in less than an hour. They had time to grab a burrito from a street vendor nearby.

It was midway through the water volleyball timeslot, so there was much action in the pool when Julia and Ricardo entered the complex. As they walked the short distance from the entrance to the activity pool, Julia spied Malcolm playing on the south side of the net, meaning that unless he turned one-eighty degrees, he wouldn't see them until he exited the pool.

In the parking lot, they had seen one of the vehicles Kate had described and were now looking for a man whose appearance she'd characterized as five-ten, medium build, with a very fit body and a full head of gray hair worn in a crew cut. Ricardo nudged Julia and tipped his head, indicating the person sitting a few feet to their left.

Julia approached him and quietly introduced herself, saying they would like to chat with him about a case they were working. It was another windy day in San Amaro. There were not many people lounging by the pools. The man, who introduced himself as Charlie Forrest, followed the officers to a vacant table away from the activity pool, where Julia began her questions.

"Do you play poker at Malcolm Davenport's regularly?" Getting an affirmative, she inquired as to how long he'd been attending the poker evenings. Julia learned that Malcolm's games usually started at eight in the evening and went until about two. He provided the names of the others who were regulars.

"Do you recall a poker game at Malcolm's old place around the second week of October, fifteen years ago?" Julia continued the questioning. Charlie asked if she was serious and upon learning she was, stopped smirking and gave the question serious consideration. Julia added that it was just before Malcolm's girlfriend at the time had moved away from San Amaro.

Charlie indicated that he might have been there, but he couldn't remember with any certainty. Julia paused for a moment and then asked if he could remember any times Malcolm had ended the poker evenings earlier than usual. This caused the man to cock his head to the side in much the same manner, Julia thought, as a dog trying to figure something out.

"He's only done that a couple of times," Charlie said after a few moments. "And one of those times was way back. It could have been fifteen years ago, but I can't be sure. It was still pretty hot. I remember that much. So, it could have been October. Malc kicked us all out before midnight, but I don't have any memory of who was there that night."

Charlie paused for a moment as though re-evaluating his last statement. Then his face brightened. "Actually, I do remember one other person who was there that night, Chu-Lee Kim. I remember because she was really pissed that Malcolm kicked us out early. She'd lost a bunch and wanted a chance to win it back."

Ricardo, who had been listening and making notes from Julia's Spanish asides to him, mentioned to Julia that the current game was almost over. Julia thanked Charlie, and he was back at his table preparing to play in the next game by the time Malcolm and his teammates vacated the pool after winning their game. Julia had asked Charlie not to mention their conversation to Malcolm, but didn't hold much hope that he'd comply.

She would contact Chu-Lee Kim to see what she remembered of Malcolm's poker games. She aimed to learn as much as she could about Malcolm from his buddies. With luck, perhaps they'd learn something they could use in future interrogations of the man.

Chapter Forty-Eight – Present Day

With every step Malcolm took on his walk home from the pools, his black mood intensified. The police car inched along the road apace with Malcolm's stride. He pushed the sky-blue door with such force that it smashed into the wall with a resonating bang, causing Callum to run into the living room to see what had happened.

"You've got some explaining to do, Cal." Malcolm spat the words at his brother. "Those stupid detectives were at water volleyball today, talking to people I play poker with. There's only one way they'd know who to talk to, and that they'd be at the pools. Someone is ratting me out to the pigs, and it has to be you, my own brother, spying on me for the cops. Get the hell out of my house, Callum. Now!"

"Now you hold on a goddamn minute, Malc. In the first place, I don't even know who you play poker with. And secondly, I haven't talked to the police since the first day I was here. I'm not spying on you! Find someone else to blame, brother. It's not me. Maybe the detectives here are good at their job. Did you ever think of that?"

Malcolm was not used to hearing Callum raise his voice. His brother was normally the calm, rational one. Cal's angry retort made him pause a moment, but unfortunately, he couldn't clear his mind enough to absorb his brother's words.

"I said, get out. I don't want you here. I thought you were on my side, that you'd protect me. I see now how wrong I was. You want the cops to stitch me up for something I didn't do, don't you? Why?

What did I ever do to you?" Malcolm quickly moved around the room, picked up a book Callum had been reading, and threw it at him. "Take your shit and get out."

Callum flinched away from the paperback projectile, and his heart felt on the point of breaking. His brother was losing his grasp on reality. He could see there was no point in trying to reason with him. Not right then, at any rate. He picked up his book and retreated to his room. He had no intention of leaving Malcolm alone with his delusions.

Callum quickly realized, however, it wasn't going to be as easy as staying in his room for an hour until Malcolm calmed down. His brother was relentlessly pounding on Callum's bedroom door, shouting at him to get out of the house. Callum finally grabbed his book and stormed out of the house amid the crazy rantings from his brother.

Callum headed to the pool complex. It was the nearest place he could sit and think. With the day's wind, he figured it would be fairly quiet there, now that volleyball was over for the day. He found a somewhat sheltered lounge chair and dropped into it. His adrenaline was still pumping from his interaction with Malcolm. Unaware of his actions, he shook his head, attempting to erase his brother's crazy rantings from his mind.

It was clear to Callum that Malcolm was not able to see his current situation rationally. Something was going on that went miles beyond a girlfriend returning from his past. The facial reconstruction that the police had shown him gave Callum the heebie-jeebies. If it was haunting Malcolm half as much as it was Callum, it could account for Malcolm's mad assertions.

Something was terribly, horrifyingly wrong. Even Callum was having a hard time believing his brother was capable of...he could hardly bring himself to even think the word. Murder.

An hour later, Callum was beginning to escape the ravaging effects of adrenaline and was able to think rationally. Whether Malcolm wanted it or not, Callum had decided he needed to hire a lawyer. If his brother wouldn't speak with one, at least Callum could find out what the police were likely going to do and, hopefully, come up with a strategy to help his brother.

Callum could see that Malcolm was becoming unhinged. Their family had no history of dementia, though Callum's wife had suffered a significant mental decline during her last three years. At that time, he'd read everything he could find about dementia. He spent part of his afternoon evaluating Malcolm's behavior against what he remembered from his research.

He'd considered that the uncharacteristic angry outbursts could signal the onset of Alzheimer's or other cognitive impairment. However, given the amount his brother was drinking and the laser-focused interest the police were showing in him, Callum feared Malcolm's descent toward madness had a more sinister beginning.

As he trudged back to Malcolm's, Callum resolved to meet the terrible fear of what he believed had happened head-on. When he entered the house, however, Malcolm was gone.

Though he hadn't done it in years, Callum prayed. *Please, God, give Malcolm the mental and emotional strength to deal with whatever he's done and me the strength to help him.*

Julia was still concerned that their evidence against Malcolm wasn't enough to get an arrest warrant for him. Even the tooth fragment, though they could prove it was Heather's, didn't prove anything about who caused her death. But for some unknown reason, Julia's thoughts returned again and again to the piece of tooth Ricardo had found in Malcolm's truck. That alone was enough for her to pay attention. Her mind was trying to tell her something.

Vicente was in the lab when she entered. He appeared to be doing a fingerprint analysis of evidence for another case. He looked up at her rap on the open door. "Is there any way to determine if the piece of tooth Ricardo found from our woman in the cistern was broken before or after death?"

Vicente rubbed the back of his neck absently. It was a habit Julia had observed in the young man when he was nervous or unsure. She quickly explained that she wondered if Heather had been in the truck after she died. Had Malcolm transported her corpse to the Filbert's cistern? Had she been killed in the truck? Or possibly died in transit?

The young man pulled a tome from a bookcase and set it on his workbench. After flipping through pages and reading for a few minutes, he looked up with a small smile. "It might be possible. Let's have a look," Vicente said.

The skull now looked very ghoulish. Much of the upper portion retained the plastina face that Vicente and Araceli had constructed. The jaw, chin, and portions of the nose had been previously scraped clean so Vicente could determine if the tooth fragment discovered in Malcolm's truck was Heather's. Now, he held a flashlight in one hand and a magnifying glass in the other as he peered into the skull's gaping maw.

"I'm trying to see if the remaining tooth stub shows signs of dentin formation. Our bodies start the healing process almost immediately upon being hurt. If there is no reactionary dentin formation, then the tooth broke at or after time of death," he said. Julia watched for several minutes while Vicente looked at the tooth from every angle, using a dentist's mirror. He finally extracted it and used a microscope to confirm his suspicion.

When his investigation was complete, he turned to Julia. "I do not see any sign of reactionary dentin. The tooth must have been broken either post-mortem or at the time of death. It would have taken a blow to the side of her jaw to cause that kind of tooth damage. The back of her head hitting the counter wouldn't have done it. Plus, Ricardo just found out that Heather was seen by the cleaner walking out of the club."

"Great, thanks, Vicente. That means Heather was likely in Malcolm's truck when she died."

Chapter Forty-Nine – Present Day

Julia had one more phone call to make to the regulars at Malcolm's poker parties. So far, she'd learned that the format of the evening games was always similar. People arrived around eight, drinks were poured, and a few minutes of shooting the bull ensued. Then, around eight-thirty, they'd start their first game. It was usually Texas Hold'em, but occasionally, they'd play five-card stud. They always played until about two in the morning.

"Hello, Mr. Wilburn?" Julia asked into the phone. Getting a positive reply, she introduced herself. "I'm not sure if you'll remember, but we spoke a little over a year ago about the murdered man on the pickleball courts. Today, I'm phoning about Malcolm Davenport and his regular poker games."

Glenn Wilburn did remember her, and that at one point, she had considered him a possible suspect in that murder last year.

"Don't worry," Julia said. "I just have some general questions. You're not suspected of anything." As she led him through her questions, his prompt answers tallied with the others with whom she'd spoken. When she asked about a game in October, fifteen years ago, the man paused for several moments before answering.

"Oh my God, I can't remember the game from three weeks ago, let alone fifteen years ago," he said with a slight laugh.

"On the night in question, I believe Malcolm cut the game short. Does that ring any bells?" Julia asked, hoping the prompt would help his memory.

"Yeah, actually, I do remember a night when he kicked us out early. It was a weird night. Malcolm is usually pretty focused on playing, and he plays well. He doesn't lose very much or very often, but that night, something was off with him. He was betting wildly, and he lost more than usual."

Glenn continued his story, mentioning that Malcolm's mood darkened as the evening passed. Initially, he'd thought it was because Malcolm was hemorrhaging money, but then he'd made a couple of odd remarks about his girlfriend, who was out for the night. From Malcolm's mutterings, Glenn said he got the idea she was seeing someone else.

"It was a side of Malcolm I'd never seen before. He was jealous…and angry. Anyway, just before midnight, he said he needed to collect her, and we all had to leave. It was very abrupt, almost like it was a spur-of-the-moment decision."

She and Glenn spoke for a few more minutes, and as she'd done with each of the other poker regulars, she'd asked about Chu-Lee Kim. She'd gotten the woman's name from Charlie, but no one had known anything about her other than her attendance at poker nights. Glenn, however, was able to procure her email address from his wife, Rhonda. He explained they played Mahjong together.

Julia had also asked each player if they'd known Malcolm's girlfriend at the time, Heather. Most did not remember her and said she hadn't been around on poker nights. Glenn was the first player to recall her. However, he said she'd been at the house only a few times on poker nights that he could remember. Then he added that she had stayed in the bedroom during the games.

It was just more circumstantial information, but Julia knew that with enough strong, logical, and interconnected circumstances, a judge might consider their case viable for a trial. She felt they were close to that threshold. She hoped they were. This cat-and-mouse game was starting to get to her.

With Dutch incapacitated, they had no other suspect than Malcolm, and their consensus was that he was involved in her death. Yet finding hard evidence was nearly impossible after all these years. In Mexico, a criminal case relying primarily on circumstantial evidence must provide the judge with a coherent, logical, and strong chain of evidence that convincingly establishes the person's guilt.

Julia firmly believed they were getting close to achieving that hurdle. When Ricardo entered the war room, Julia polled his opinion on that topic and learned he had already begun a conversation with Inspector Martinez about it.

"I think it's time we present our entire case to Hector," Ricardo said. "It will be good preparation for presenting it to the judge, and he'll let us know if our evidence and all the circumstances we can describe are sufficient to get an arrest warrant."

With that as their plan of action, the pair began to pull together everything their investigation had produced into a timeline, a witness statement summary, and a description of Malcolm's actions. They had all the information available in their war room, but turning it into a compelling and convincing story would take some time.

Chapter Fifty – Present Day

Ricardo and Julia had spent two days preparing their case against Malcolm. They had finally received the DNA results from the blood found at the club. Now, armed with a steaming mug of coffee, Inspector Martinez joined them in the war room to adjudicate their presentation. If convinced, he would take the case to a representative of the *Ministerio Público*, the Public Ministry, who reviews charges and determines if there is sufficient evidence to proceed. Together, they told the inspector their story.

On the fourth of February of this year, the police were alerted to a skeleton discovered in a cistern at a property in the Cortez Oasis community. The place had been vacant for sixteen years but had recently been listed for sale. The autopsy revealed the deceased was a Caucasian woman in her fifties, dead for approximately fifteen years. A hard fall against a sharp-edged surface had broken a cervical vertebra—the ultimate, but not immediate cause of death.

A facial reconstruction was made from the skull, and posters were placed all over town and in the predominantly expat communities north of town. The woman's identity was eventually uncovered as Heather Holstaff. Further investigation uncovered the name of Heather's boyfriend at the time of her death, Malcolm Davenport.

Davenport had owned a home near the location where the remains were discovered, but had moved to a different house miles away, still in the same community, a few years after Heather's death. The day the photos of the facial reconstruction were posted, Davenport left San Amaro and drove to La Paz. Ten days later, the police tracked him down using GPS data provided by his cellular carrier and returned him to San Amaro.

The last time the victim was seen alive, she was preparing to leave the Cha-Cha Club at two in the morning on October 9, 2010, in the company of Malcolm Davenport. Witnesses indicated he was very drunk. The Club has been permanently closed for most of the last thirteen years, but a forensic examination there turned up Heather's blood on the underside of the sharp-edged counter in the women's bathroom.

A woman who used to be the Club's cleaner admitted to seeing Malcolm and Heather in the women's bathroom after closing on the night in question. She thought they were having sex because Malcolm was helping Heather off the floor.

Friends of the deceased who were partying with her that night said they danced with some guys who were passing through San Amaro on a motorcycle trip. One mentioned a possible sighting of Malcolm at the door of the Club about an hour before closing. Malcolm might have been waiting for Heather outside the club prior to closing. It was possible Heather had used the bathroom before heading home.

An investigation of Davenport's truck turned up two pieces of evidence. The first was an earring that matched both the earring found near the remains and a photo showing the victim wearing those earrings taken at The Club the evening she disappeared.

The second was a tooth fragment missing from a broken molar in the skull. Forensic analysis of the tooth revealed a complete lack of reactionary dentin formation on the root of the tooth, indicating it was broken at or after the time of death.

Interviews with his brother and past girlfriends revealed that Malcolm was initially a very attentive romantic partner. However, his attentiveness eventually turned to jealousy and anger as his imagined betrayal by his girlfriends often resulted in physical violence.

Given the evidence and witness statements, the most probable scenario is that Malcolm and Heather had had an altercation in the bathroom, resulting in Heather falling against the counter and cracking her cervical vertebra, and that she died in Malcolm's truck on the drive home.

The coroner indicated that a sharp movement of Heather's head after the fall would have been necessary to cause the cracked vertebra to shear, killing her instantly. Otherwise, it would have taken longer for her to die than the twenty-minute drive from the club to their house. Given the earring and the broken tooth fragment, it is likely Malcolm had punched or slapped her in the truck, resulting in immediate death.

Martinez gave the pair an appraising look when they reached the end of their case.

"Are you hoping for a charge of murder or manslaughter?"

Chapter Fifty-One – Present Day

"Since the hurdle for murder is intent to cause death, I think the best we can hope for is manslaughter," Inspector Martinez said finally. The three had discussed several factors that could influence the decision. The components affecting the decision included more than just intent. Aggravating factors, such as advantage, needed to be considered.

Julia argued that Malcolm had such an advantage over Heather—a larger, stronger man versus a small woman—and that they could try for the lesser *homicidio califacado*, something akin to second-degree murder in the United States. Hector and Ricardo didn't think they were likely to convince a judge to write an arrest warrant for the lesser murder charge, but Hector said he'd give it a try.

Since they were not sure a judge would see their evidence as sufficient for even the manslaughter charge, Hector secretly liked the idea of trying for homicidio califacado first. He would argue Julia's point about advantage, and if that didn't work, the judge might be more likely to opt for manslaughter than nothing. It was worth a try.

Martinez had booked a meeting with the Public Ministry representative, the equivalent of an American Attorney General, for the next afternoon. But before he returned to his office with Julia and Ricardo's report, photos, and his additional notes from their morning discussion to prepare, he raised a lingering concern he harbored.

"I wish there was some way we could positively rule out that Dutch character as a suspect," Hector said. "Julia, I want you to stay in touch with the hospital in Denver. If there is any chance for a phone conversation with him when he comes out of the coma, I want to be sure you finish your interview with him about his actions after leaving the club."

After Hector returned to his office, Julia found the phone number for Saint Joseph Hospital. After finally being connected to the ICU, she learned that Dutch had been moved from the ICU to a private room but had still been uncommunicative when he left the ICU. The nurse with whom she had been speaking tried to transfer her call to the appropriate nursing station, but Julia got cut off.

On her second attempt, Julia had more luck. This time, she asked for the nursing station attending to Dutch and was finally connected with someone who knew the man's current status. His physical injuries—a broken left arm and several broken ribs—were slowly mending. His head trauma, however, was still an issue. He was out of the coma, and his ability to form coherent sentences was improving.

The nurse recommended calling back the following day.

Chapter Fifty-Two - Present Day

Inspector Martinez told Julia he wanted to interrogate Malcolm again before he went to the Public Ministry. He had rescheduled his appointment two days ahead. He wanted the interview with Malcolm to happen the following morning. Julia had much work to do in preparation. She headed home to work on her assignment. It had been a decade since she'd completed her undergraduate degree in psychology, but she'd never gotten rid of any of her textbooks. Today wasn't the first time she'd pulled them out for a case.

She reread her note on the main characteristics of people with an entitlement mentality, jealousy, and difficulty regulating anger. If she could get inside Malcolm's head, she might be able to manipulate him into admitting what he'd done. Even if she couldn't achieve that goal, she might still be able to get enough information from him to make a second-degree murder or manslaughter charge stick.

As she read, Julia made notes on specific situations that would likely evoke highly emotional responses from Malcolm. In his past interviews, Malcolm had been adamant he was innocent of whatever the police thought he'd done. Julia needed to bombard him with indicators of the falseness of his assertions. She needed to rock his foundational belief that he was a nice guy, continually being wronged by the women he dated. She had to make him see his true behavior to break down his façade of geniality and expose the selfish abuser at his core.

As Julia developed a few scenarios she planned to use and the roles her fellow officers needed to play in them, another thought flickered through her mind. *What if Malcolm was losing his grip on reality? Was it possible that his firm belief that he hadn't done anything wrong was a delusion he believed was the truth?*

With those thoughts in mind, Julia returned to her textbooks as well as scouring the internet for information on interrogating someone who was not in their right mind. By the end of the day, she was convinced that the upcoming interview with Malcolm would likely be the hardest interrogation she'd ever undertaken.

After dinner, she went to talk with her grandfather. She laid out the situation for him and asked him to critique her planned approach, citing Malcolm's potentially fragile grip on reality as a concern. Juan's first thought was how much his granddaughter had matured as a detective over the last four years.

He was impressed with her plans to wrench her suspect out of his comfort zone using her background in psychology. He had nothing to add in that arena. He was able to provide her with his knowledge of cases where insanity might play a part.

She left feeling confident in her ability to do this interview.

Chapter Fifty-Three – Present Day

Julia's first action of the morning was to call Saint Joseph's Hospital in Denver. Once she was connected to the right desk, she inquired about Warren Bakker's ability to answer some questions. The nurse transferred Julia's call to the phone in Mr. Bakker's room. Moments later, a deep baritone voice answered in a querulous tone.

"Mr. Bakker, this is Detective Sergeant Julia Garcia calling from San Amaro. Do you remember speaking with me just before your car accident?" Getting an affirmative answer, she plowed ahead.

"If you recall, I was asking you about your actions after you and your friends left the Cha-Cha Club on the last night of your time in Baja. Can you answer that now for me, please?" It was phrased as a question, but Dutch realized his response was not optional.

Though his speech was slow and faltered occasionally, Julia did not doubt that the man was lucid. He described leaving the club and walking the three blocks to the hotel where he and his friends were staying. His description matched the one his roommate, Len, had given Julia the previous week.

"Did you leave your hotel room again that evening after you and Len returned from the club?" Julia asked.

"No… I didn't." Dutch spoke slowly, his enunciation sloppy as though he were drunk.

"After Len was through in the bathroom… he climbed into his bed and was asleep… before I was finished digging… my toothbrush out of my… luggage."

"Just take your time Mr. Bakker." His breathing was sounding labored, as though the effort of talking exhausted him.

"I was about… five minutes behind him in getting to sleep. Tell me again… why you're asking me about that night?"

Julia told him that the night in question was the last time anyone saw Heather alive. She'd been murdered.

"Holy shit," Dutch said, then paused as though taking in what he'd just heard. "Did I know that… before? Did you tell me when we spoke… before?"

Julia assured him she'd told him before. The more she talked with him, the less she thought he was involved in Heather's death.

"That is really sad. She seemed like… a nice woman. It's not like I really knew her. We basically… just danced together. Awful to imagine… she was killed."

Julia had a few more questions, but none of Dutch's answers caused her to change her view that he wasn't involved.

She left a note on Inspector Martinez's desk saying Dutch was no longer a viable suspect. Then she and Ricardo left the station to go collect Malcolm. It was time for his interrogation.

Chapter Fifty-Four – Present Day

Callum had been avoiding Malcolm by staying sequestered in his bedroom. For his part, Malcolm had been staying out of the house by spending more time at the brewery. Consequently, he was drunker more often than his previous, already high level of intoxication. When a loud knocking, coupled with 'Police, open up', shattered the early morning calm, Callum went to the door. He knew Malcolm would not be awake yet.

Ten minutes later, a groggy but fully clothed Malcolm was loaded into the back of the cruiser. Callum had spoken to his brother through his bedroom door while they waited for him to dress. "I'm hiring a lawyer for you. No matter what you say."

The response from behind the closed door left Callum shaking his head. "Don't waste your money. I'm innocent."

Malcolm was placed in Interview Room Two. It was already fitted out with cameras and microphones that transmitted to Ricardo's desk and through the translation software installed on his computer. Once again he would watch and listen to the interview in Spanish. With Malcolm settled in the interview room and Luis standing guard, Ricardo and Julia met with Inspector Martinez to finalize their plans for the upcoming interrogation. Julia had warned Luis about what he could expect during the interview and how she wanted him to respond.

Callum had joined one of the local Facebook groups expats used in San Amaro and asked for recommendations on local Spanish and English-speaking lawyers. Given the answers he got, he decided either there were not many such lawyers in town or the one name that all the respondents provided must be exceptional. He'd called the number as soon as the police had taken Malcolm. He'd left a message and impatiently awaited a return call.

When the call finally came through at ten that morning, Callum picked it up in the middle of the first ring. He explained that his brother was being interviewed by the police, for the second time, in conjunction with the woman in the cistern. The lawyer, Jennifer Ochoa, said to meet at her office on the Malecon at eleven. Armed with directions, Callum promised to be there.

The first twenty minutes in the barren room, Malcolm waited impatiently, trying to keep his mind clear and alert for the start of his interview. The effort of trying to stay focused proved either too difficult or too boring. Malcolm placed his crossed arms on the table, lowered his head to his arm, and fell asleep.

Though Luis had not attended many interrogations, he found the behavior strange and a little unsettling. It was, however, a pleasant change from the man's voluble rantings about his innocence. The Spanish word, inocencia, was close enough to the word Malcolm shouted to be very clear to Luis what the man was claiming.

Callum explained to Jennifer Ochoa the little he knew of the case in which his brother appeared to be the prime suspect. She was familiar with the case in general, as it was still hot news in the small town. As she probed deeper into the story, Callum realized he knew even less about it than he'd realized.

"I will need to speak with Malcolm before I can properly represent him," Jennifer said.

"That might be difficult. Malcolm continues to say he doesn't need a lawyer," Callum said. Seeing Jennifer's querying expression, he continued. "I know. It's crazy. And I'm using that word intentionally. I think Malcolm is losing his mind. It may be the onset of dementia, or maybe he's just cracking up with the stress of the situation. I don't know. What I do know is that Malcolm is not himself. He's acting crazy. I don't know how else to describe it."

Saying it out loud made it all too real for Callum. Emotion and worry swept over him, and he struggled to maintain his composure. A few moments passed before he finished his thought. "I need you to help me understand the implications for Malcolm if he is going crazy and if he does get charged with this crime. I get the impression the police think it was murder. Is there anything I can do to help my brother?"

Malcolm was still sleeping when Julia and the inspector entered the room. As agreed, Julia started strong. She dropped her thick file folder for the case on the table, causing a loud smacking sound. Malcolm flinched and jerked his head from his arms.

"Sit up." Julia commanded. It startled the inspector and Ricardo, whose ears were still recovering from the dropped folder sound reverberating through his headphones.

"Can I get a Coke?" Malcolm asked, though it sounded more like a demand than a question.

"No. I'll give you a bottle of water when you earn it by telling me the truth." Julia sounded like an army drill sergeant. "Your brother must be so disappointed in you. Running to him for protection. I'll bet he's spent his life cleaning up your messes."

"Leave Callum out of this. He knows I haven't done anything."

"That's not what he told me, Mr. Davenport," Julia said.

"You're lying. He always had my back. You bring him in here. I'm not saying another word until you bring Callum here." Malcolm leaned back in his chair. He crossed his arms over his chest. A small smirk curled the corners of his lips.

"You don't control this situation, Malcolm. I do." Julia had never started an interview in such a confrontational manner before. It made her uncomfortable, but she knew their best shot at getting this man to talk was to agitate him sufficiently to break through his fantasy belief that he hadn't done anything to Heather.

"Now start talking."

Chapter Fifty-Five – Present Day

Jennifer Ochoa's law practice on the Malecon sat between a tourist shop with T-shirts and floaties and a taqueria. By small-town Mexican standards, it was a plush office. Carpet rather than tile was the first thing Callum noticed. Almost no place in San Amaro had carpeting. The entry area contained a reception desk with two chairs fronting it, a couch and coffee table against one wall, and a beverage counter with a single-serve coffee maker and bottled water.

After offering a choice of beverages, which Callum declined, the receptionist led Callum through to the lawyer's office. Jennifer Ochoa was an attractive woman in her mid-forties. She was of average height, with shoulder-length, jet black hair, and brown eyes so penetrating, Callum had no doubt the woman before him knew her stuff. He relaxed slightly for the first time since the police had shown up at his door in La Paz.

At Jennifer's request, Callum provided a detailed description of everything he'd witnessed since Malcolm's arrival in La Paz. He reiterated Malcolm's initial explanation of why he'd left San Amaro, but said that, witnessing Malcolm's excessive drinking, he quickly realized that his brother was lying to him.

When the police had shown up to transport Malcolm back to San Amaro, Callum realized something serious must have happened. He explained that he'd driven Malcolm's SUV to San Amaro and described his first meeting with the police.

At Jennifer's prompting, he told her of his reaction when the police showed him the photo of the facial reconstruction. "I realized that I'd seen that woman's photos on Malcolm's Facebook from years before. I didn't tell the police that, but seeing it, I finally understood that the police thought Malcolm had murdered her. I don't know what evidence they have on him, but they took him back to the station this morning."

Next, Jennifer had Callum describe Malcolm's behavior and explain why he thought his brother's mental faculties might be declining. She took many notes as Callum itemized how Malcolm's behavior now was different from his past actions. When Callum was finished, Jennifer sat back in her chair and glanced over her notes before returning her intelligent, penetrating eyes to Callum.

"Why don't you believe your brother's assertion that he's innocent?"

Callum was taken aback by the bluntness of the question and stunned into silence by its implication. He finally spoke.

"I never said that I think he's guilty. I can't imagine Malcolm ki…killing someone."

Jennifer's gaze never left his face. "You obviously think he's guilty of something, or you wouldn't be here."

"What I want from you is an understanding of how the Mexican legal system handles people who are not fully *compos mentis*. Because I don't think my brother is in full control of his mind. I don't think he's taking the police's interest in him seriously, and I don't know what to do to help him. Don't you understand? I just want to help my brother, and I don't know how."

Callum looked as though he were about to cry.

"Can you help him, or not?"

"Mr. Davenport, I have spoken to two of your previous girlfriends. They paint a pretty clear picture of what it's like to be in a relationship with you. They described you as possessive, controlling, jealous, and, when you didn't get your way, you became physically aggressive. One said you slapped her so hard she momentarily blacked out. The other said you punched her. You have a history..."

Malcolm stood up so fast, he almost knocked over the table between him and the police. His face was purple with rage.

"Those bitches! The only reason I got angry with them was because they weren't loyal. Women always sneak around like cats in heat. The minute your back is turned, they're going out with someone else. That would make anyone jealous."

Luis and the inspector were both on their feet and at Malcolm's side in seconds, each holding an arm. Martinez pressed down on Malcolm's shoulder, getting him seated again. His angry voice rasped in broken, accented English. "You sit stay, or handcuffs."

Julia continued.

"Here's what we know, Mr. Davenport. The last time anyone saw Heather alive was in the wee hours of the morning of October 9, 2010, leaving the women's bathroom of the Cha-Cha Club with you. We have reports that you were very drunk, and Heather needed support to walk." Julia began to provide the evidence the police had on Malcolm.

Malcolm took in a deep breath as though to begin speaking, but Julia stopped him.

"Shut up. You need to listen to what I'm telling you. We have all the evidence we need to charge you with Heather Holstaff's death, so don't interrupt me again. You'll get your chance to talk later. When I tell you, you can talk."

Julia was being intentionally abrasive, and it was having the desired effect on Malcolm. His face was flushed, his fists were balled, and his body was as tense as a support cable on a suspension bridge.

"Heather's skeleton was discovered in a pile at the back of a cistern at the abandoned home of Jeremy and Rosemary Filbert, less than a quarter of a mile from where you were living fifteen years ago. From our investigation and the evidence we've collected, we know what happened, Mr. Davenport."

Julia then detailed every piece of evidence they collected and the story it told. She left the finding of the broken earring and tooth fragment in his old truck until the end. "We know Heather was alive when you two left the club, and we know that when Heather fell in the bathroom and hit her head, she damaged a vertebra at the top of her neck.

"Because of the earring and the tooth fragment, we know that Heather died in your truck that night. But here's the kicker, Malcolm. That vertebra only sheared in two because something struck her jaw with enough force to break a tooth. The broken fragment found in your truck tells us you hit her. Hard enough to break a tooth and to cause the vertebra to shear, causing her death."

Malcolm lifted his balled fists in a menacing pose and leaned forward in his chair, scowling at Julia. Luis stepped forward to place a hand, none too gently, on his shoulder, causing Malcolm to sit back.

"The fact that the stub of the broken tooth that remained in the jawbone showed no sign of something called reactionary dentin means she died within seconds of being struck. She was alive when she got in your truck at the club and dead by the time you arrived at your house. You killed her, and we have all the proof we need to charge you with her death.

Something approaching a growl was emitted from deep in Malcolm's throat.

"Now it's your turn, Mr. Davenport. What do you have to say?"

Chapter Fifty-Six – Present Day

Jennifer Ochoa felt the anxiety wafting from the man across the desk. He had provided what information he knew, which wasn't much. And he expected her to inform him of the options open to his brother's defense for a crime for which he had not yet been arrested. Callum had told her that his brother didn't want a lawyer, and she was not being given any opportunity to speak to the brother to get his side of the story.

"Well, Mr Davenport, I'm not sure how much good I can do you. But, I can tell you how Mexican law handles non-imputability, which is how it refers to mental incapability. I believe in the US, a person can use an insanity defense."

"Yes, that's it. Please carry on, this is what I need to understand."

"In Mexico, one must prove that at the time of the crime, the perpetrator was incapable of understanding or controlling his or her actions. Given that the crime occurred fifteen years ago, I doubt that anyone could prove your brother's mental state at the time of the crime. Especially if he had been perceived as normal," she used air quotes to delineate the word, "in the intervening years."

Callum let out a long, sad sigh. He sounded like a man defeated. The lawyer continued, in the hope of providing him a lifeline.

"The other option in a criminal trial is a defense of mental incompetence at the time of the trial. That is only considered if the defendant's mental state prevents them from standing trial due to a psychological condition."

Callum sat forward as though to speak, but the lawyer continued before he could.

"I'm sure the two things sound the same." Callum nodded his head dejectedly. "But the former refers to the person's mental state at the time the crime was committed. The latter relates to the mental state of the defendant at the time of the trial. In Mexican law, a person must be deemed capable of understanding the proceedings for a fair trial."

"How is that determined?"

"If we can prove that your brother has diminished mental capacity now, he might be considered incapable of standing trial. For example, if he were diagnosed with dementia or Alzheimer's, and it was determined, by a psychiatrist, that he would not be able to understand the trial proceedings, the charges might be dropped. That doesn't usually happen in a case of murder. The other options would be for your brother to be remanded to the Instituto de Psiquiatría del Estado de Baja, in Tijuana. It's a forensic psychiatric hospital for criminals."

"Oh God. I don't know which is worse."

"Beyond that information, I don't know what else I can do for you." Jennifer spread her hands, palm up, in a gesture of helplessness.

"You've been very helpful. This is the information I need to know. I'm going to try to convince Malcolm to speak with you and hire you as his lawyer, if you're willing to take on his case."

Jennifer nodded that she was.

"Do you know if there is one of those forensic hospital places near La Paz? I'm there half the year."

Jennifer smiled. "Yes. There's one in La Paz."

"You people are nuts. You're trying to stitch me up for something I didn't do. I didn't kill that woman. You've fabricated evidence and made up a story, but none of it is true. I picked up Red from the club, and I drove her home. She told me she was leaving. And the next morning, she packed up her car and left. I haven't seen her since. End of story." Malcolm leaned back in his chair and crossed his arms over his chest.

"Well, Mr. Davenport. We know you did it. So I suggest you spend some more time in a cell, and we'll talk again later." Julia nodded to Luis, who had been standing sentinel by the door. He helped Malcolm stand and led him toward the back of the station. Malcolm tried to brush Luis's hand away from his arm and shouted abuse at the young constable. For his part, Luis gripped Malcolm's arm harder as he moved the man into a cell.

Chapter Fifty-Seven – Present Day

Callum drove straight to the police station from the lawyer's office. He told the desk sergeant he wished to speak with Detective Sergeant Garcia. It was not long since Julia had ended her interview with Malcolm, so she was available. She joined Callum in the foyer, and once she learned he wanted to speak with his brother, she placed him in the interview room his brother had only recently vacated.

Before Julia left the room, Callum asked. "Is it possible to speak to him privately?" She looked at the man solemnly.

"Mr. Davenport, in Mexico, you don't have any legal right to speak with your brother." She paused momentarily, then added, "We do, however, have discretion in allowing it. I will permit you to talk together, but there is no promise of privacy in a police station. I will either be in the room with you or observing from another office."

"I understand."

Julia informed Ricardo and the inspector of Callum's presence and desire to talk with Malcolm. The three debated whether Julia should be in the interview room with them while the brothers talked, or if they should only watch and listen from Ricardo's desk.

Martinez said he wanted to be in the room with them and that Julia and Ricardo should observe from their desks. Once everyone was in place. Julia retrieved Malcolm from his cell, telling him only that he was being allowed to speak with his brother.

Callum had feared that he and Malcolm would not be able to talk confidentially and had the forethought to buy a pad of lined paper from a store near the Malecon. He'd written notes he wanted to give to Malcolm. He suspected that in the best-case scenario, that the police would read them. At worst, they'd be confiscated before Malcolm could read them. Callum was willing to take that risk.

"What are you doing here? Don't you get it? I don't want your help. And I don't need your help. I haven't done anything wrong." Malcolm's greeting was not what Callum had hoped. Although he wasn't overly surprised. Malcolm's belligerent attitude had become the norm in their interactions.

"You need to be quiet and listen to me, Malcolm. This is important. I've just met with a lawyer and there are some things you need to know. Read this before you say anything else. When you've finished, I hope you'll see why you must hire her."

Malcolm reached out for the pad, but Inspector Martinez stepped away from the door to retrieve the papers before Malcolm. Julia had anticipated his action and was waiting outside the interview room when Martinez emerged with the notes. She read through Callum's pages. His poor penmanship caused her to read more slowly than normal. When she finished, she realized that Callum's thinking about his brother was along the same lines as hers.

Callum's notes talked about the onset of dementia, mentioning angry, irrational outbursts, and argumentativeness, and describing Malcolm's corresponding behaviors. They also outlined what he'd learned about imputability due to psychiatric issues in Mexican law. The notes also contained a plea that Malcolm hire a lawyer and ended with the reassurance that he would stick by his brother through whatever was to come.

Julia described the details of the letter to the inspector. Together, they decided to let Malcolm read it and see where things went after that. When she handed the pages to Malcolm, she added her own thoughts. "Mr. Davenport, I recommend you take your brother's words seriously. He has your best interests at heart."

Malcolm took the pages, and for a moment, it looked like he was going to read them. The next instant, however, he balled them up and threw them at Callum. "Are you on their payroll, you traitor? You're just a backstabber. You don't have anyone but your own interests in mind. I keep telling you, I'm innocent, and all you're doing is proving to me you think I'm guilty."

Malcolm turned away from Callum, toward the inspector and Julia. "If you're not going to let me go, then take me back to the cell. I don't want to have this turncoat near me."

Julia gathered the crumpled pages from the table, then walked Malcolm back to the cells. As she placed him inside, she handed him his brother's letter. "I strongly suggest you read this, Mr. Davenport. Your brother is not helping us in any way. We have interviewed him twice, but he hasn't provided us with any damaging information about you. He really is trying to help you. There is good information there. I hope you'll at least give it your consideration."

Chapter Fifty-Eight – Present Day

Inspector Martinez had asked Callum to remain in the interview room because Julia needed to speak with him before he left. When she returned from parking Malcolm in a cell, she took the seat previously occupied by Malcolm. Looking across at Callum, she could see the toll his brother's situation was causing him. The man looked a decade older than when they'd spoken at Malcolm's home.

"Mr. Davenport–" Julia began.

"Please call me Callum."

"Okay, Callum. Thanks for staying. I want to talk to you about the concerns you expressed in your letter to Malcolm. In addition to being a police officer and having studied criminology, I also have a degree in psychology. In my limited time with your brother, I've seen evidence that made me wonder if his mental health was faltering. So, I'm glad to see that you've been speaking with a lawyer about how mental incompetence might be a factor concerning the charges for which we plan to arrest him."

At hearing those last words, Callum leaned forward anxiously. It was as though he hadn't fully grasped the severity of the situation Malcolm was in, or he had fooled himself into believing, or at least hoping, that his brother was just a witness. Julia spent several minutes recounting all the evidence the police had against Malcolm. When she finished, it was clear that Callum fully understood the desperate situation Malcolm was in. It appeared to age him another decade.

"What I need from you is an understanding of why you think Malcolm is losing his mind, to put it informally. It may impact how we proceed with the case against him. And, for the record, I strongly encouraged him to read your notes and give them serious consideration. However, if he is losing his mental faculties, he may not be able to see your words positively. Rather, he may view them as more evidence of your duplicity. So, please help me get a better understanding of how Malcolm has changed."

Callum stayed in the interview room with Julia for almost an hour. He outlined what he described as Malcolm's normal demeanor and then juxtaposed it with the depressed, angry, drunken man with whom he'd been living for the past few weeks. It was a sad tale. One that left Callum depleted and raw.

For her part, Julia mostly just listened, letting the man ramble through memories, recent and past. He finished his monologue with a question that Julia had been expecting. "So, what happens to Malcolm next?"

"Before I answer that, I have a question of my own. Do you think Malcolm knows what happened and his part in it, and is hoping that if he professes his innocence convincingly, he'll get away with it?"

Callum took several moments before he responded. Julia watched emotions play out on the man's face and waited.

"You seem like a good cop, Detective Garcia. I have to admit, I was expecting something very different from Mexican police. I'm sorry to say, I wasn't expecting such a thorough investigation, the humane treatment Malcolm has received, or your apparent desire to ensure Malcolm is given proper care if he needs it. Thank you for changing my bias. I'm not trying to avoid your question. I honestly don't know how to answer."

"Perhaps you can explain your dilemma to me so I can better understand," Julia said.

Callum smiled a sad smile and shook his head in either agreement or resignation. "As a kid, Malcolm had a history of lying to save his skin. Never for anything serious. And I don't think that's so unusual in teenage boys. And while I know he likes to be able to blame others for the issues in his life, I think what's happening now is something different than trying to save himself."

"Different in what way? Please give me more details to help me understand."

"I think what he needs is a proper psychiatric evaluation to find out if he is experiencing some kind of mental decline. I've also wondered if his inability to come to grips with what he's doneis what's driving him mad. Either way, I think a professional evaluation of his mental condition should be done. What do you think?"

Julia knew what she wanted to say, that she agreed, and that it was what they planned to do. But it wasn't her call to make. "Whether your brother gets the kind of testing you're suggesting is a matter for a judge to determine." She explained that the Public Ministry representative is the person to whom the police present their evidence and who then determines the next steps. In Malcolm's case, that could be authorizing the arrest or ordering a psych eval.

"If you're willing, I'd like to have a transcript typed up of the salient parts of our conversation just now to be included, along with my notes, in the information we present to the Public Ministry.

Inspector Martinez already has an appointment set up to present our case against Malcolm.'

I don't understand the idea of the Public Ministry. Who or what is it?"

"The Public Ministry is similar to the US District Attorney's office. Someone from that office will decide what actual charges are filed. Inspector Martinez will speak with the representative of the Public Ministry, and your comments will be most relevant to that person. Do you agree to us using your own words to influence the charges?"

Callum agreed readily.

Martinez and Ricardo had been listening to Julia and Callum's conversation and were waiting for Julia in the war room after she had escorted Callum out of the station. Their discussion focused on the question of Malcolm's sanity and whether or not it should be a factor in Martinez's presentation to the attorney general.

Ricardo's stance was clear. "I want him to stand trial and go to jail if he's guilty. I think those psych hospitals are a cop out."

"But the law is clear that if he can't understand what is happening at a trial, he can't be tried," Martinez countered.

"We're not going to get anywhere with this debate without a professional determination of his competence." Julia chimed in with her opinion.

After some lively debate, a consensus was reached that the judge needed all the information they had amassed, including Callum's concern that Malcolm might have Alzheimer's or other dementia related disease, or that his inability to cope with what he'd done had driven him crazy.

Julia and Ricardo spent the remainder of the day updating the presentation that Martinez would make to the Public Ministry the following day.

Before she left the station for the day, Julia stopped by Malcolm's cell. He was asleep on his bunk. Julia was glad to see the pages from Callum's letter had been smoothed out and were in a neat pile on the floor beside the bunk. She hoped he'd read them.

Tomorrow was sure to be an interesting day for this case.

Chapter Fifty-Nine – Present Day

Inspector Martinez returned to the station after his meeting with the Public Ministry and called Ricardo and Julia, who were anxious to hear the decision on how to charge Malcolm. The air in the room was electric with anticipation.

Martinex didn't keep them waiting. "The attorney postponed any charges against Mr. Davenport until a psych eval is performed. A psychiatrist is coming tomorrow from Instituto de Psiquiatría, the criminal psychiatric hospital in Tijuana, to do the evaluation." Ricardo's eyebrows shot up in surprise at how quickly it would begin.

"The evaluation process will likely take a few days," Martinez said. "In addition to interviewing us and Malcolm, he'll want to interview Callum, some of Malcolm's friends, and review any criminal history Malcolm has. Please organize and schedule the interviews with the brother and a person or two from his day-to-day life. I would like us to be interviewed first, to give him context. Callum and Malcolm's friends can follow our interviews. That will take all of tomorrow. Malcolm should likely be the last interview."

Martinez returned to his office to make sure everything he needed to share with the evaluator was in order. Julia and Ricardo got busy with their tasks. It was the first time either of them had been involved in a criminal psychiatric evaluation. They were equal parts excited and nervous about the process.

Julia started by calling Callum. She told him the decision of the Public Ministry to have a psych eval done and outlined the process of interviews and testing that would occur. She also encouraged him to hire a lawyer to assist Malcolm through the process. Once Callum's interview time had been set and his questions answered to the best of Julia's ability, Julia had one final question for him.

"Do you think I should tell Malcolm that he's going to be evaluated by a psychiatrist, and what to expect, or just let him experience it with no forewarning?" It was something she was truly concerned about. Malcolm seemed to be becoming more unhinged and less able to cope, as witnessed by his assertions that he'd done nothing wrong, even in the face of the overwhelming evidence against him.

Callum sighed deeply into the phone. "I'm not sure. Do you have any thoughts on the situation?"

"Honestly, I think it would be better not to give him advanced warning. That way, the evaluator will experience Malcolm's unprepared reaction. However, if you have a strong feeling not to do it that way, I would like to hear it, so we can consider it in our final decision."

Callum did not have a contrary opinion. Julia asked if he had any other questions or concerns. When Callum said no, she ended the call by reiterating the time Callum was expected at the station the following day. She also told Callum the day and time Malcolm would need representation, if Callum were to hire a lawyer.

Next, Julia called a friend she had in the Phoenix Police Department. Jesus del Toro had been in a few of Julia's criminology classes when she was getting her master's degree. They'd had a brief fling but determined they were better as friends and had stayed in touch after graduation. She had his cell number and called him directly rather than calling the station. As it turned out, Jesus was in the station house when he answered her call.

Julia briefly outlined the case she was working on and explained the need for a criminal record report from the States on Malcolm Davenport. She provided the man's full name and US Social Security Number. After a few moments, Jesus gave her a verbal report and emailed the complete report to her. It appeared the only time Malcolm had been in trouble with the law was a drunk and disorderly charge in Alaska from the early 1980s.

The pair spent a few minutes catching up before ending the call. Julia then turned her attention to finding a few of Malcolm's friends who were willing to be interviewed for his psych eval.

Immediately upon hanging up from his call with Julia, Callum dialed the number for Jennifer Ochoa's law office. When he was put through to the lawyer, he gave her the news. As far as Callum was concerned, it was good news, even great news. The cops weren't going to charge Malcolm until it had been determined if he was fit to stand trial. Jennifer was also optimistic. And, to Callum's relief, she agreed to represent Malcolm through the evaluation process, as needed.

Callum was quite sure that Malcolm would not agree to pay for a lawyer, since he'd been so adamant that he didn't need one. However, he wasn't going to allow his brother to face the legal system neither of them understood, alone. He would cover any legal bills. The retainer requested by the lawyer was a fraction of what it would have been in the US. Callum was grateful. His finances provided him with a comfortable, if modest, life. He didn't have extra thousands of dollars lying around.

Chapter Sixty – Present Day

Doctor Mateo Mendoza arrived at the San Amaro State Police Station just before noon. He'd driven from his office in the Instituto de Psiquiatría. The desk sergeant escorted him to Inspector Martinez's office. The two men had not previously met, and each took the measure of the other as they shook hands. Martinez placed the doctor's age to be early forties. Younger than he'd expected, but the man had a stellar reputation.

"Is this your first time in San Amaro, Doctor Mendoza?" asked the inspector.

"No, no, not at all. I am originally from Puertecitos, so my family came here often. It has grown since I was a boy. Are you from here?"

"My wife is," Martinez said. "I am from about as far from here as you can get, Chetumal, on the East coast, not far from Belize. Would you like some lunch before we get started?"

The two men continued getting to know each other over lunch and returned to the station shortly after one. Contrary to Martinez's plans to have the psychiatrist interview Malcolm last, Dr. Mendoza said he'd spend an hour or more with Malcolm before interviewing anyone else. Martinez phoned Julia to change the needed appointment times she'd previously set up. The inspector requested that the conversation with Malcolm take place in an interview room, allowing him and his team to observe via the existing audio and video setup. The doctor agreed.

Malcolm was brought from his cell to the interview room, where Dr. Mendoza waited. Ricardo had relocated his computer, which had all the translation software and connections to the interview room equipment, to the war room. He, Martinez, and Julia watched with anticipation as the evaluation began. However, what they watched was more like small talk between acquaintances than a psychological or psychiatric evaluation.

An hour later, Mendoza thanked Malcolm and signaled to the camera in the top corner of the room that he was finished, and someone should escort Malcolm back to the cell. Julia took care of Malcolm and then joined the doctor and the others in the war room. Of his initial time with Malcolm, Mendoza said only that it was sufficient to get a baseline.

Next, Dr. Mendoza said he wanted to speak with Callum and that he wanted to do it in Malcolm's home, if possible. Julia phoned Callum and got an affirmative answer, so she taxied the doctor to the Oasis in La Chica. On the drive, Mendoza indicated he wanted to speak with Callum alone, so after dropping him at Malcolm's house, Julia headed to a nearby coffee shop to wait for his call.

Callum answered the door promptly. Mendoza introduced himself and was invited to have a seat at the kitchen table. Callum offered coffee and some pastries from the local convenience store. Dr. Mendoza took a coffee, black, but passed on the snacks.

"Tell me about your brother, starting from when you were kids." The doctor pulled out a notebook and leaned back to listen.

Callum had some trepidation about being interviewed by the shrink, but Mendoza's manner was friendly and warm. Callum felt safe with this man. It surprised and disarmed him. He opened up immediately, sharing stories and insights into his brother as a child that he'd all but forgotten.

Mendoza provided prompts when Callum appeared to be winding down. When the doctor stood to leave, Callum was surprised to realize that the man had been there for almost three hours. "Did you get what you needed?" Callum was aware that all his hopes for Malcolm's future rested on the results of this man's evaluation.

"Thank you, you were very helpful," Mendoza answered cryptically.

Julia's car was idling in front of the house. She was glad she'd brought her computer with her. She was able to get some work done at the coffee shop during her waiting time. She noticed he held a tattered old book, like a journal or diary. She didn't recall seeing it when she dropped him off.

Once he was in the car, her question to the doctor was almost identical to Callum's. His answer to her was also the same. After a curt, "Yes, he was very helpful," Mendoza turned to look out the car window, effectively curtailing any further conversation.

Julia drove in silence. *He lives up to his name*, she thought. *Mendoza* means cold mountain. He was certainly built like a mountain. His broad shoulders overlapped the car seat, and his head all but brushed the headliner. His brisk response left a coolness in the air between them.

It was the end of Julia's shift when she and Mendoza arrived back at the station. She was ready to be rid of the silent mountain, so she was startled when he asked if she'd join him for an early dinner. She didn't have any plans for her evening and thought she might be able to learn something from the man. She agreed.

Twenty minutes later, after Julia had dropped off her computer and given a brief update to Inspector Martinez, she and Mendoza were back in La Chica heading to a steakhouse Mendoza had heard about in the ejido north of town. Julia knew of it but had never been there. All she knew was that it was very expensive.

The drive to the eatery was the complete opposite of their previous trip. As they climbed into the car, Mendoza was like a new person. "Sorry if I seemed rude before. It's just part of my approach. I needed some quiet time to process my interview with Malcolm's brother," he said in a warm, cheery tone. "My name is Mateo, by the way. I hope you're okay with dropping the formal titles, at least for this evening. Is it alright if I call you Julia?"

"Absolutely," Julia said, smiling inwardly at herself. She needed to revisit her snap evaluation that he was a cold mountain. He seemed like a nice man. By the time they reached the restaurant, Julia was delighted to be in his company. Before they entered, she pulled the scrunchy from the bun at her nape and shook out her hair.

Mateo had chosen a Tempranillo from Chile, which Julia found to be bold and delightfully earthy with hints of cherry and a slightly spicy finish. Once the wine was poured, Julia ordered a filet rare while Mateo opted for the ribeye medium rare. Both chose the baked potato and grilled veggies to round out their meal.

They shared origin stories as they waited for their meals. Julia revealed the loss of her father to a car accident when she was sixteen, her unfortunate relationship with her mother, and herself as an only child. She also admitted what had been causing her a heavy sadness for days—that her phone call might have been a contributing factor in Dutch's car accident. *Thank godness he was going to be okay.*

From Mateo, she learned he was a native of the Baja Sur town of Puertecitos, a very small town about an hour south of San Amaro, though he'd lived and worked in Tijuana since graduating with his degree in psychiatry. He was single after losing his wife three years into their marriage to metastatic breast cancer.

They chatted easily, each comfortable with the other as though old friends. Julia found Mateo's square-jawed face open and inviting and could imagine it helped encourage his clients to open up to him. It was his eyes, however, that held her attention. They were soft brown, and gentle, fringed with dark lashes for which any woman would pay good money.

After their dinner plates were cleared away, Mateo ordered flan with two forks and two snifters of brandy.

"I'm curious what drew you to choose psychiatry," Julia said.

"Well, I always wanted a medical degree because I wanted to help people be well. I got into forensic psychiatry for some of the same reasons you chose policing. I think justice is critical in holding a society to a standard of equality, fairness, and impartiality. If people perceive that laws and institutions that enforce them are just, they're more likely to respect and abide by them."

Julia agreed. "Yes, that certainly matches my belief."

"Did you know that the rights of individuals with mental issues charged with a crime weren't codified into law here until 2010? Before that, people with mental issues convicted of a crime were incarcerated in prisons. And, it wasn't until just a couple of years ago that Mexican criminal law was updated to align with international human rights. I've been an advocate and activist in getting politicians to understand the issues and change our laws. Thank God, they finally did."

Watching him speak with such passion about his career touched Julia. She saw him as a gentle warrior who was driven by empathy and humanity. “Yes, thank goodness for them.” She placed her hand on his. “And thank goodness for you, for fighting for it in the first place.”

She smiled, then removed her hand. It was an unconscious act of intimacy. Her ease in doing it caused her mind to snap to attention. When had she last felt this comfortable with a man? She couldn’t remember. But she remembered the feeling…and liked it.

Chapter Sixty-One – Present Day

Dr. Mendoza arrived at the station at exactly eight o'clock the next morning. Julia met him in the foyer, and together they joined Ricardo and Inspector Martinez in the war room. A bag of donuts and other pastries sat in the middle of the table. Upon seeing a single cinnamon bun on a napkin beside the bag, Julia determined that Ricardo was responsible. He alone knew of Julia's near obsession with cinnamon buns. She flashed him a smile in acknowledgement and thanks.

Martinez started the meeting off by reading the report Julia and Ricardo had prepared the previous week for the judge. He felt it concisely described the situation of finding human remains, the investigation performed by Julia and Ricardo, and the actions taken by Malcolm Davenport. Julia had a folder of photos, including the facial reconstruction and evidence collected, and she placed them on the table one at a time to better illuminate the narrative.

"Thank you, that was a very good overview of the situation," the doctor said. "Now, let's get into the details."

For the next four hours, Mateo asked them ever more complex questions, evoking increasingly detailed answers. Some of the questions were easily answered, others drew the officers into deep self-reflection.

When did you first suspect that Malcolm was delusional? What behaviors did he exhibit in later interviews that you hadn't noticed initially? Did Malcolm's story of the events of Heather's departure change over time? What was your impression of the relationship between Malcolm and his brother? What experience have you had with persons with dementia that might be clouding your judgment?

Julia found the process equal parts exhausting and energizing. Exhausting because of the mental effort involved, and energizing because of the insights she gleaned by observing Mateo's process. He was clearly a brilliant person and, by Julia's reckoning, very good at this job.

Julia had scheduled interviews with Glenn Wilburn and Ray Lomand, both poker buddies and fellow water volleyball players with Malcolm. She was in the foyer when Glenn arrived and delivered him to Interview Room Two, where Dr. Mendoza waited.

"How long have you known Malcolm Davenport?" Dr. Mendoza asked once the formal interview began. When he learned that the two men had been friends for more than eighteen years, the doctor asked a series of questions about what Malcolm was like during the first couple of years of their friendship and whether his behavior changed after Heather was no longer living with him. The questions went on from there.

In the end, three things made it into the doctor's notebook:

1. Malcolm had started to drink more around the time of Heather's death.
2. In the year and a half before he met Heather, Malcolm had a string of short-term girlfriends. Since Heather's death, Malcolm had not dated anyone.
3. About three years ago, Malcolm became increasingly moody, easily angered, and paranoid that his friends were spying on him.

Dr. Mendoza had about thirty minutes before his interview with Ray Lomand. He used the time to read the transcripts of the police interviews with Malcolm and Callum. He'd received them via email before coming to San Amaro, but he found rereading them now provided some additional insights. Two more observations went into his notebook.

4. Malcolm's sense of entitlement appears to absolve him of taking responsibility for his actions.
5. In conflict with #4, Malcolm has a clear sense of right and wrong. It is producing cognitive dissonance.

Ray Lomand's interview was much shorter than Glenn's. Mendoza focused his questions on the past five years and any differences Ray noticed in Malcolm's behavior during that time. Only two things stood out to the doctor. He added them to his list.

6. About three years ago, Malcolm's ability to deal with difficulties decreased markedly. He became quick to display anger or frustration.
7. Malcolm's poker prowess began to decline in the past year.

Dr. Mendoza met up with Julia and Ricardo in the war room once he was finished with Ray's interview. They were preparing to leave for the day. He didn't provide any feedback on how his interviews had gone beyond saying he was getting the background he needed and was on track to begin cognitive testing with Malcolm in the morning.

He asked the pair what they thought about allowing Malcolm to spend the night at home rather than in a cell. He suggested that Malcolm might be in a more natural, relaxed state for the testing if allowed to sleep in his own bed. Inspector Martinez was consulted and gave his approval.

Julia retrieved Malcolm from this cell and was about to take him out to La Chica when the doctor blocked their way. “Mind if I join you?” he asked Julia. “Or I can just speak to him a minute before you go, if you prefer.”

Julia’s breath caught for a moment before she answered. “Sure, come on.” She turned away quickly so he wouldn’t see her blush.

Mateo surprised her further by sitting in the back seat with Malcolm. It soon became clear that Mateo wanted to come so he could talk with Malcolm. Julia mentally shook her head with embarrassment over thinking he’d asked to come along to be with her.

Mateo was speaking softly, and Julia could only make out some of the conversation. When they pulled up in front of Malcolm’s home, Mateo joined Julia as she escorted Malcolm inside. With Callum present, Mateo gave Malcolm instructions. “Tomorrow is going to be a full day for us. I want you to get a good night’s sleep and have no more than two drinks tonight. Got it? You will need to have a clear head tomorrow. We’ll come pick you up in the morning at eight-thirty.”

Malcolm and Callum acknowledged the doctor’s directions. Julia and Mateo returned to La Chica. As they left the Oasis, Mateo spotted the brewery and suggested they stop for a beer. “That’s a great idea.” She crossed the highway and turned into the brewery parking lot.

Their easy rapport from the previous evening continued as they enjoyed a delicious craft beer. It was a lovely fall day, with warm temperatures and a gentle breeze, so the pair opted to sit at one of the outdoor tables with excellent views of the sea.

As it was Mateo's first time at the brewery, he was delighted to see a food trailer in the outdoor space. He wandered over to peruse the chalkboard menu. When he returned, he placed a small yellow triangle with the number twelve displayed on two sides on the table. "I took the liberty of ordering us some dinner. Menudo and empanadas. I hope you don't mind, and I hope you like my choices."

"That's perfect. Thanks."

Julia liked this man from Tijuana.

Chapter Sixty-Two – Present Day

Julia and Ricardo arrived at Malcolm's house at the appointed time and were relieved that Malcolm was ready to go. The pair was also relieved that his curmudgeon-ness was not in evidence. Julia thought back to the previous afternoon and mentally acknowledged to herself that he'd been pleasant then, too. She wondered why.

"Where's that doctor fellow? I thought he was coming to get me?" Malcolm asked from the back seat once they were underway.

Julia told him that the doctor was at the station preparing for their day together.

"Oh, good." He leaned back into the seat and was quiet the remainder of the drive.

His comment made Julia wonder if Malcolm was looking forward to the evaluation testing. The thought perplexed her as Malcolm had been so defiant every time they'd talked with him.

She ran her thoughts back to the initial conversation Mateo had with Malcolm and realized that the two men had developed a rapport during that hour. Her admiration of Dr. Mendoza increased as she recognized his talent for making people comfortable and relaxed in his company.

When Ricardo and Julia entered the station with their charge, the desk sergeant instructed them to take Malcolm to Inspector Martinez's office. As they passed the war room heading toward their boss's office, they spied Martinez working at a computer in the conference room. Ricardo popped his head in the door to inquire if they should leave Malcolm there, and learned that Dr. Mendoza was using his office for the day.

Mateo had set himself up on the round table in one corner of the inspector's office, and Julia noticed several testing aids she had learned about in her undergraduate psychology courses. Despite their budding friendship, Mateo was all business when thanking Julia for getting Malcolm.

Malcolm entered the office and offered a hand to Mateo. "Hi, Doc."

After a couple of minutes of pleasantries, Mendoza got down to work. He started with a five-minute Mini-Mental State Exam, which consisted of several simple questions to determine Malcolm's awareness of his current situation. *Where do you live? What is today's full date? What's the name of the place we're in today?*

"Okay, next, we're going to play a memory game. I'll tell you three words and you repeat them back to me, okay?" Malcolm nodded, and Dr. Mendoza continued. "The words are quiet, photo, and whisper. Can you repeat them for me, please?"

Malcolm paused for a second and recited in a strong, clear voice. "Photo, whisper, um…," his voice wavered, but seconds later, he added, "and quiet." A smile crossed his face. He knew he'd gotten all three right.

"Great. Now, let's see how you are at arithmetic. What's one hundred and four minus seven?"

When Malcolm provided the correct answer, the doctor requested that Malcolm continue to subtract seven from each subsequent answer. Malcolm screwed his eyes shut as though he were trying to see the numbers on a mental blackboard. When he pronounced forty-eight as the eighth result, Mendoza moved on.

On the otherwise clear tabletop were several items. Mendoza moved them in front of Malcolm and asked him to identify each in turn. When that exercise was complete, he asked Malcolm to repeat the three words from the previous test.

"Photo, whisker, and, erm...shit, I can't remember the last one." Malcolm's mood up until this point had been open and relaxed; however, his inability to remember the last word flipped a switch in the man's demeanor. Instantly, his face darkened. He swore under his breath and pushed back from the table.

"Let's move on to something more fun," Mendoza said as he, too, pushed his chair back from the table. He gave Malcolm a warm smile and placed some blank paper on the table with a variety of pencils and pens. "I want you to draw a clock showing eight-fifteen. Use whatever writing implement you wish."

Malcolm selected a blue pencil crayon and drew a circle. Next, he put a dot in the center. After changing to a red pencil, he added the hour and minute hands before sliding the paper across the table to the doctor.

Mendoza was relieved that Malcolm's dark mood had passed. The drawing exercises had brought him back to a more neutral state of mind. "Okay, next, I want you to copy this diagram." He placed a line diagram of two intersecting rectangles in front of Malcolm.

After several more drawing exercises, the doctor removed everything from the table and announced that next, he'd gather some medical information. In addition to asking general questions about Malcolm's health, he checked his reflexes, his eye movements, and his balance. He concluded the medical testing with some questions to help assess Malcolm's self-awareness of any mental decline, and a few to evaluate his ability to apply logic.

How often do you have trouble remembering people's names? Is it harder now than it used to be? Have you ever forgotten a pot on a lit burner? What does the saying 'The pot calling the kettle black' mean? How are an apple and a banana alike? If you found a stamped, addressed envelope in the street, what would you do with it?

As it approached lunchtime, Mendoza could see Malcolm was getting tired. "Okay, let's end there. You've done really well to stay focused all this time, I'll bet you're feeling a bit tired. Hey, do you remember any of those words from this morning?"

Malcolm tipped his head back and looked at the ceiling for a moment. "I remember 'photo' but not the other two. I know they weren't things, you know, like not physical things. Oh yeah, one of them was 'whisper' and the last one was something like that too, but I don't remember it."

A half hour before, Mateo had texted Julia to let her know when Malcolm would be finished. Their plan was to have Callum come to the station and bring the lawyer he'd hired for the afternoon. Callum was aware of this, and when he received the call from Julia, he contacted Jennifer Ochoa with the time she needed to be at the station.

Callum arrived at the station just a few minutes before Dr. Mendoza ushered Malcolm into Interview Room Two. When Malcolm entered, he was greeted with a platter of enchiladas with rice and beans, and a bottle of Topo Chico. The same meal was in front of Callum. Dr. Mendoza left the brothers to enjoy their lunch and went to the war room, where Martinez, Julia, and Ricardo waited.

They didn't have long to prepare for the next and likely final component of the psych eval. This afternoon, they'd confront Malcolm again with all the evidence they had in the case against him. This time, Dr. Mendoza would be in the interview room to observe and make suggestions to the interviewer, if needed. Also in the room would be Jennifer Ochoa, Malcolm's lawyer.

For the three police officers at the heart of this case, the coming afternoon held great importance. Dr. Mendoza's evaluation report, along with the recording of the upcoming interview, would be the final pieces in the case. If Malcolm were ruled fit to stand trial, imputable, this would be the police's chance to test the strength of their evidence. However, if he were determined to be unimputable under Mexican law, today might mark the last chapter in the case of the woman in the cistern.

Chapter Sixty-Three – Present Day

Interview Room Two was crowded. Dr. Mendoza and Julia sat on one side of the table, while Malcolm and Jennifer Ochoa sat on the other. Malcolm and his lawyer had been given the room a half hour before to confer, though Malcolm still maintained he didn't need a lawyer.

The interview began with the standard check-in initiated by Inspector Martinez, who then took up position in much the same spot Luis had, by the door. Julia provided a brief prologue to the actual interview, primarily so that the recording being made could stand on its own in court, if needed.

"This interview forms the final component and wraps up the psychological evaluation being performed by Dr. Mateo Mendoza on Malcolm Davenport." She looked to Martinez, who gave her a brief nod, indicating she should begin. Next, she looked to Dr. Mendoza for similar approval. He also nodded.

"Mr. Davenport, do you know why you're here?" The question had been provided to Julia by the doctor.

"Of course I know. You all think I had something to do with Red's death. That's just a bunch of malarkey. You're trying to stitch me up for something I didn't do."

Jennifer Ochoa had placed a hand on Malcolm's arm while he was speaking and spoke over him. "Please don't answer unless I give you the go-ahead." Malcolm scowled at her.

"Here's the evidence, Mr. Davenport," Julia spoke in a calm, even tone. She listed each piece of physical evidence they had gathered, then went on to enumerate his telltale actions—moving, leaving town within twelve hours of the facial reconstruction photos being posted everywhere, and his historical pattern of jealousy-driven physical abuse with girlfriends.

The whole time Julia was speaking, Malcolm's lawyer did her best to restrain her client's angry outbursts. It seemed to be a losing battle.

Julia continued undaunted. "Malcolm," she intentionally used his given name in hopes he'd calm himself enough to listen to what was coming.

"Here's what we think happened in the wee hours of October nine, twenty-ten. You waited outside the Cha-Cha Club for your girlfriend, Heather Holstaff, to leave. You were seen by the club's front door about an hour before closing, though you didn't go in. As an aside, that is typical stalker behavior. When the club closed, you met Heather outside the front doors, then followed her back inside. She went into the women's restroom, and you followed."

Julia glanced at her notes to be sure she wasn't missing any pertinent details.

"There was an altercation during which Heather fell against the sink's countertop, fracturing her C1 vertebra. A cleaning lady witnessed you helping Heather off the floor. Then you were seen walking out together. That was the last time anyone saw Heather alive."

Dr. Mendoza jotted a quick note on the pages before him.

"In your truck on the drive home, your anger caused you to strike Heather on the left cheek. That action broke a tooth and ripped her left earring from her ear. Both the tooth fragment and the earring were found under the floor mat of the passenger footwell of your truck.

"The strike is what killed Heather, as it caused the fractured disc to shear, severing her spinal cord. You knew that the Filberts hadn't been to their home near yours in over a year and that the probability of them returning was very low, so you dumped Heather's body into their cistern. And dumped her car and belongings somewhere far from here."

Malcolm moved restlessly in his chair and cleared his throat as though about to speak. His lawyer leaned toward him and whispered something in his ear. When the lawyer leaned back, Julia continued.

"At some point, likely because of a hurricane, the lid of the cistern broke. Your solution was to brick it over with a small patio. Your flashlight was seen flickering around in the dark of night by one of your neighbors.

"Then, twelve years ago, you moved to a different house a few miles from your old place. I suspect the guilt over what you'd done was eating at you. Your poker buddies all remember you starting to drink more heavily than usual about that time. They also noted that your poker prowess started to decline."

Julia stopped and took a drink of water. She also wanted to create an obvious break in the interview. Jennifer Ochoa took the opportunity to again whisper something in Malcolm's ear. Julia watched them intently, perhaps trying to intuit what she was saying. Then her attention was ripped away as Dr. Mendoza's breath caressed her neck in advance of a few whispers of his own.

Julia was momentarily flustered but recovered quickly. She hoped the inspector hadn't noticed the deep blush that heated her face. She acknowledged Mateo's suggestion with a curt nod to hide her embarrassment, though it was not something she'd ever asked a suspect in an interview.

"How do you feel about what I've just said, Mr. Davenport?" Feelings were not something normally discussed during a murder investigation.

"I'm confused by it all. It's like you're talking about someone else, not me. I didn't do the things you're saying."

Julia said nothing in reply. She looked to Dr. Mendoza and, with the slightest lift of an eyebrow, turned the questioning over to him.

Mateo fished around in his briefcase for a moment, then dropped a tattered black diary on the table in front of Malcolm. At seeing it, Malcolm's eyes grew large.

"You stole this from me?" He spat across the table, looking back and forth between Julia and the doctor. Not sure which one he was accusing.

"We had a search warrant, Mr. Davenport. We didn't steal it," Julia said evenly.

She picked up the book and opened it to a previously flagged page. "Please read the passage starting here." She pointed to a paragraph dated 10/9/2010.

Malcolm looked pleadingly at his lawyer, but she indicated he should read it.

"Red (Heather) and I got home late that night after she'd been out with her girlfriends. I had gone to pick her up. On the drive home, she told me she was leaving me the next day. I wasn't ever that serious about her, so it wasn't a big deal to me. She packed up her clothes and loaded them in her car, and the next morning she left. I ain't seen her since. I called her a few days later to make sure she was okay, but the phone must a been turned off or something."

"That could easily be a simple diary entry, if it weren't for the following entry. Written with the same pen and sloppy writing, and you'll note that there is no new date associated with it. She continued reading.

"A few weeks later, she called me from a different number to say she was settled in a new place and was working as a bartender. She never said where she was, but it sounded like she was at a party or working at the bar with lots of loud people."

"Please tell me the date of the next entry in your diary, Mr. Davenport." Julia's voice was now commanding.

"It's the next day, October tenth."

"Thank you. Now, can you please tell us how you knew that Heather would move away, get another job, and another phone just hours after you picked her up at the Cha-Cha Club?"

The doctor placed his hand on Julia's arm to keep her from continuing. "Malcolm, why do you suppose you wrote this the day Heather died?"

"I, I do…I don't know," Malcolm said.

"Remember this morning, one of the games we played was to try to decipher the intended meaning of certain adages. Let's try another one along the same lines. If I told you that someone else had written something like that on a day something traumatic happened, what would you think their reason might be?"

Mendoza had prepped Julia and the inspector that he'd work the psychological angles during this interview, so neither was surprised that he'd taken over the questioning.

Malcolm dragged a hand over his stubbly chin as he thought. "They're probably trying to cover something up," he said some moments later.

"Is that what you were trying to do, Malcolm? Cover up what you did to Heather?" Mendoza's voice was soft, hardly louder than a whisper. Everyone in the room was silent, waiting.

All eyes were on Malcolm. It was clear the man was struggling. His brow alternately scrunched and released. His eyes were darting back and forth. At one point, he started rocking in his chair. His breath was coming in short pants, then suddenly the pants turned into sobs. When he balled his hands into fists and started punching himself on the thighs, Julia and the inspector moved to his sides and gently restrained his arms until he stopped fighting against them.

Mendoza waited until Malcolm had calmed somewhat. "This is clearly distressing to you, Malcolm, but I do need you to answer my question. "Were you trying to cover up what happened to Heather?"

A single trembling breath wracked Malcolm's body before he lifted his eyes from the diary to the doctor's face. A single tear trailed down his cheek. "I don't know. I just don't remember. I don't even remember going to the club to pick Heather up."

"Okay, what do you remember from that time?"

"I remember making the patio at the Filberts. And I remember crying while I did it. So, I guess what she said," he pointed to Julia, "must be what happened. I've believed for so long that this," he held up the diary open to the passage he'd just read, "was the truth. I can't get my head around any of it. I would never intentionally hurt anyone. I'm not that kind of man. I guess I go a little crazy when women are unfaithful. There's no loyalty anymore. Why?"

Julia almost felt sorry for the man; he seemed so lost and bewildered. *Or*, when the image of Heather's skeleton carelessly discarded in a cistern crossed her mind, *he's a good actor*.

Dr. Mendoza leaned over toward Julia again to whisper in her ear. This time, she was ready and managed to keep from blushing through sheer willpower. When he leaned back into his chair, she turned off the recording equipment and spoke.

"Malcolm, we're going to leave you here for a few minutes. You and your lawyer have privacy. There will be an officer outside to escort you to the bathroom if needed.

Martinez, Mendoza, and Julia vacated the room and regrouped in the war room, where Ricardo was already seated. The doctor took a few moments to review notes in his journal before addressing the three officers.

"I have enough information on Davenport to be able to complete my evaluation. From my observations of him and his performance on the tests earlier, I was ready to recommend incarceration in a forensic psychiatric hospital. Observing his responses in the interview, I am even more confident in my diagnosis. He is not capable of going to trial. What are your thoughts?" he asked.

Martinez spoke first, saying he would support that evaluation. Julia and Ricardo both began speaking as Martinez finished. Their boss interjected. "Ricardo, you first, then you, Julia."

"So what exactly does that mean? Is he going to be charged with the crime, but not tried in court, just shuffled off to a nut house? Oh, sorry, Doc, no disrespect meant."

Martinez leaned forward in preparation to answer, but Mendoza beat him to it.

"The next thing that happens is I submit my report to the same judge from the Public Ministry who requested the evaluation, and your boss will submit your report at the same time in a special judicial hearing. The judge then rules on whether or not Malcolm is fit to stand trial. You know what happens in that situation."

Mendoza asked if Ricardo had any specific questions he could address. "I just want to understand what happens if the ruling is non-imputability."

"If the ruling is non-imputability, then there will be a further ruling on whether a crime took place and, if so, whether the accused did it. Assuming both those things are found to be true, the judge determines the best course of action. In most cases, that is hospitalization, with stipulations regarding length of incarceration, changes in mental health, and anything else the judge decides."

Mendoza gave a small shrug. "Did that answer your questions, Ricardo?"

"Yeah, I guess so. It sounds like the case is out of our hands now. It feels pretty unsatisfying." Ricardo reached for his ubiquitous coffee mug and took a long drink before setting the mug down with enough force to slosh coffee onto the table. "Sorry." He grabbed a tissue from his pants pocket to sop up his mess.

Julia was nodding her head in agreement with Ricardo's last remark. "I agree, Ricardo. It feels so unsatisfactory, yet I agree that Malcolm probably doesn't have the mental capacity to stand trial. So, from a humanitarian perspective, a hospital makes the most sense."

Having had the chance to air her disappointment, Julia moved on to the practical. "So, what do I tell Malcolm when we get back downstairs?"

Martinez and Mendoza coached her on the proper terms to use when describing the next steps to Malcolm. Martinez also had the date for Malcolm's judicial hearing with the Public Ministry.

Chapter Sixty-Five – Present Day

Martinez had heard the frustration expressed by Julia and Ricardo about the likely outcome of Malcolm's appearance in front of the Public Ministry judge. He had, therefore, arranged for the pair to escort Malcolm to the hearing and observe the process. Besides alleviating some of their angst, he'd reasoned, it was a good learning opportunity for them.

Fortunately, the San Amaro Public Ministry was not as swamped as Mexicali's or Tijuana's, so Malcolm's hearing was only two days after Dr. Mendoza completed his psych eval. As a result, the doctor had decided to stay in San Amaro rather than return to Tijuana, only to have to be back in San Amaro a day later.

He could have let Martinez present his evaluation. But there was every chance that the judge would want to question him about his evaluation of Malcolm. Besides, it gave him a couple more opportunities to spend time with Julia.

The courtroom where Malcolm's hearing was being held was small and seemed even smaller once everyone was assembled there. Callum, Julia, Ricardo, and Dr. Mendoza were seated in the pew-like benches behind a small railing. Malcolm and Jennifer Ochoa sat at a small table in front and to the left of the slightly raised platform with a larger table where the judge sat. To the right of the judge sat Martinez with the member of the Attorney General's office who would be prosecuting Malcolm.

The presiding judge was the same person Martinez had presented his team's report on their case against Malcolm. He had also formally requested Malcolm's psychological evaluation, so he was familiar with the case in general terms.

The hearing would be conducted in Spanish, but since the suspect was not a Spanish speaker, Malcolm had been assigned a court-appointed interpreter. Julia watched Malcolm intently. He appeared to be very uncomfortable, squirming in his chair and wildly looking around the room like a caged animal. His lawyer was doing her best to calm him. She was having limited success.

Callum had also noticed Malcolm's behavior. The judge had not yet entered the room, so he slipped from his seat and went to the railing directly behind his brother. Julia watched as Callum placed a steady hand on his brother's shoulder, then bent forward to speak softly to him. She had no idea what was said, but Malcolm appeared to settle down.

As Callum returned to his seat, the bailiff, or *Actuario Judicial* in Mexico, called the hearing to order, and the judge entered. Once everyone was settled and the initial formalities performed, the judge described what would happen at the hearing.

Three things needed to be determined: Was a crime committed? Did the defendant commit the crime? Is the defendant imputable, capable of standing trial, and understanding the proceedings?

The coroner's report was entered into evidence to confirm that a crime had been committed. It indicated that though Heather Holstaff had accidentally hit her head, causing a disc fracture, a subsequent blow to the head, administered by the defendant, caused the bone to shear. The result was instant death.

The charge against Malcolm was manslaughter.

He then had the prosecutor address the second question. Had the case presented by Inspector Martinez the previous week against Malcolm convinced him of Malcolm's guilt? The prosecutor indicated that it had. The state believed that Malcolm's actions had hastened Heather's death.

The remainder of the hearing was spent determining if Malcolm's mental state was imputable. Dr. Mendoza was called to the stand. He was asked to describe the testing methods he used and how Malcolm's performance on those tests had led the doctor to his findings.

Mendoza was on the stand answering the prosecutor's questions until the judge stopped the proceedings for their lunch break. As he stepped down from the stand, Julia could see the toll the hours-long examination had taken on him.

The doctor joined Ricardo, Julia, and Martinez for lunch. They found a quiet table in a pizzeria near the courthouse.

"How do you think it's going?" Martinez asked once they'd ordered.

"It's clear the prosecutor is looking for anything that might indicate Malcolm has faked his responses, trying to avoid jail," Mendoza said. "But I don't think the judge has been convinced that Malcolm is lying."

Chapter Sixty-Six – Present Day

The hearing resumed with the prosecutor asking a few final questions of Dr. Mendoza. "You've already stated that you believe Mr. Davenport has experienced a psychotic break. In your professional opinion, what caused this to occur?"

"Mr. Davenport is exhibiting many signs of dementia, though he is in the early stages of the disease. That is a contributing factor in his current mental state. And it will continue to erode his mental capacity as the disease progresses. However, in my opinion, from my conversations with Mr. Davenport, his grip on reality began eroding from the time he disposed of Ms. Holstaff's body in the cistern.

"Over the ensuing fifteen years, he has not been able to accept that he caused her death. Part of his mind has tried to shield him from that reality by creating the myth that she left him, while another part agonizes over the fact that he did cause her death."

He went on to provide examples, in Malcolm's own words, from the transcripts of his evaluation. It was clear to those in the courtroom that Malcolm carried conflicting beliefs about what happened the night of Heather's death. At times, he resolutely maintained that Heather had moved out and left San Amaro. At others, he railed against her for not being faithful to him, saying she deserved what she got.

Mendoza described a man whose mind was shattered.

Julia watched Malcolm intently during Mendoza's description of his mental state. It was clear that having the proceedings translated in short bursts was difficult for him. He appeared very confused and angry during most of the hearing. Several times through the hearing, as Malcolm's outbursts disrupted proceedings, the judge had to remind Jennifer Ochoa to keep her client quiet. She was trying desperately to do just that, but Malcolm was not complying.

The judge retired to his chambers to deliberate once Mendoza was finished testifying. Those in the courtroom shuffled in their seats. No one knew how long the judge would take. The quiet rumble of whispered conversations soon filled the space as they waited.

Almost an hour later, the *Actuario Judicial* announced the judge's return. Silence swept the room. There was a palpable tension while they awaited his verdict. Julia found herself holding her breath.

Malcolm was mumbling to his lawyer and needed to be shushed before the judge provided his verdict.

Unimputable.

Malcolm would not be standing trial.

The judge outlined his recommendation that Malcolm be incarcerated in the state psychiatric hospital in Tijuana for ten years, the hospital where Dr. Mendoza worked. During that time, his mental state would be reevaluated annually to determine the progression of his dementia using the Clinical Dementia Rating Scale. Currently, Malcolm was rated a 1.

He would be kept at the hospital for ten years or until his dementia was severe enough to require help with basic tasks like dressing and feeding himself. At that point, he'd be released into a qualifying public facility for the remainder of his life.

Malcolm's lawyer asked if Malcolm could serve his time in the psychiatric hospital in La Paz, as his brother lived there. Jurisdictional issues kept the judge from fulfilling that request.

As they were leaving the courthouse, Mendoza spoke with a dejected-looking Callum. "There is a process by which you can request a transfer for Malcolm. Once he's in the system and settled in Tijuana, you can file the paperwork to have him moved to La Paz. I have a colleague who works in the La Paz hospital. He and I can do our best to expedite a transfer, but it may take a few weeks."

The news visibly improved Callum's demeanor, though it was obvious to Julia that the man was struggling with the whole idea that his brother had killed someone and covered up his crime.

Malcolm was to be transported to Tijuana the following day. Two constables escorted him from the courtroom into a waiting squad car. The trip to the police station was only a few blocks. He would spend the night in a cell in San Amaro. Callum left Mendoza and caught up with Julia.

"Will I be able to see Malcolm this afternoon? Dr. Mendoza said he can take his own clothes and a few toiletries and personal items to the hospital. I'd like to speak with Malc to find out what he wants to take. Is that possible?"

Julia indicated that she would make sure the brothers had time together later that afternoon. There were some formalities to be taken care of now that Malcolm's case had been adjudicated. They agreed Callum would come to the station at three that afternoon.

Julia's eyes scanned the small knot of people standing outside the courthouse and finally spied Ricardo chatting with Martinez and Mendoza. She joined them. She mentioned her arrangement with Callum and suggested to Ricardo that they get back to the station to complete the required paperwork.

Before she and Ricardo departed, she spoke briefly to Inspector Martinez. "Can Ricardo and I get some time with you later today? I… I… I just need to debrief this case." It was obvious to her boss that the usually unflappable Julia was frustrated with the outcome of the case. He agreed.

Julia's mind was buzzing as she tried to clarify to herself why she was so agitated. Ricardo could see she needed to be alone with her thoughts. It was a silent drive back to the station.

Chapter Sixty-Seven – Present Day

Julia pulled up a chair in front of Malcolm's cell. The man was sitting on the cot, eyeing her with suspicion. "What the hell do you want?" he said. His voice was gruff, but gone was the haughtiness that characterized her previous interactions with him.

"Malcolm, do you know what happened today at the courthouse?" Her tone had a pleading note to it. It surprised her, and it grabbed the man's attention.

"That doctor guy, Mateo," Malcolm said. "He thinks I'm crazy. And he convinced the judge of that, too. So, you're going to lock me up, right?" He sent Julia a challenging look.

"Well, here's how I see what happened. Mateo doesn't think you're crazy, and neither do I. But we both know that your mind isn't working properly. You know what dementia is, don't you?"

"Of course, I do." His feistiness returned, if only for a moment.

"You are showing early signs of having dementia." Malcolm began to argue, but Julia held up a hand for him to stop and carried on. "Today, the court pronounced you guilty of causing, at least in part, Heather's death. As well as covering up your crime. But because of Mateo's evaluation, the judge determined that you are not mentally able to stand trial for those crimes. Do you understand all that?"

"Didn't I just stand trial?"

"No, that was a hearing to determine if you were capable of standing trial and understanding the proceedings. You will spend ten years in a state hospital for people like yourself, who are incapable of having a trial. What do you think of that?"

"So, I'm going to a hospital instead of jail?"

"Yes, that's right."

"But I never meant to hurt Heather. I just needed her to stop making that awful moaning sound. I didn't…mean it. She went quiet. I didn't realize. Then, when I opened the truck door, she was gone. Her eyes were just…" His voice trailed off, and his gaze drifted, unseeing, to a place just over Julia's shoulder and a time, she guessed, that was fifteen years prior.

It was as close to a confession as Julia was going to get. She trudged upstairs to help Ricardo with the paperwork.

Inspector Martinez strolled into the war room close to quitting time. "Are you ready to debrief this case?"

Julia told Ricardo and Matrinez about her conversation with Malcolm. "So, you got a confession of sorts. Did that change anything for you?" her boss asked.

"Yes. I needed to hear him say he was involved."

She went on to express the frustration she'd felt in trying to prove Malcolm's involvement in Heather's death. "Even with all the evidence against him, I wanted to hear him admit his part. Then, as I started to realize that he might not be in control of his faculties, I didn't want to prosecute him if he couldn't understand what was happening. This whole case, since we discovered Heather's identity and Malcolm's involvement, has left me feeling very unsatisfied."

Ricardo and Hector Martinez looked at each other, then back at Julia. Neither man had previously witnessed Julia being so vulnerable and unsure of herself.

Martinez marshaled his thoughts. "I understand that this has been a frustrating outcome, but let's look at the case. You two started with an old skeleton in a cistern. You learned from the coroner that it was a woman, and the physical actions that led to her death. Then you discovered the identity of the remains. Found witnesses. Learned the identity of Malcolm. And you found evidence supporting the fact that Malcolm was involved." He paused, looking meaningfully at Julia.

"Through your investigation, you began to worry that Malcolm was not mentally capable of a trial and helped ensure a psych eval was done. The imputability hearing determined you were correct in your concern. The evidence you two collected and the report of your investigation were sufficient to convince the judge of Malcolm's involvement in Heather's death. And he will be incarcerated in a place where his dementia can be handled professionally. What part of this has left you feeling frustrated? From where I stand, it seems like an excellent outcome to a difficult case."

Julia slowly nodded her head.

"You're right, of course. There isn't a better outcome than this, given all the facts. I'm glad I spoke with Malcolm earlier. It really helped me to hear him admit he was involved. And thank you, Hector. I appreciate how succinctly you described the overall case. I'm okay…" The war room phone cut short the remainder of her response. Callum was in the foyer.

Julia found the man looking at posters of criminals on the corkboard to the left of the entry door. She invited him to sit with her for a few moments.

"I spoke with Malcolm a few minutes ago, and he admitted his involvement in Heather's death. He seems to have some idea of what's happening, but I'm sure he'll be glad to see you. I see you have some things for him. He can't have them while he's in the cell here. But I will ensure he gets them when he leaves for Tijuana tomorrow. Did you have any questions for me before I bring him out for you two to talk?"

"No, I think I'm okay. Mateo explained a few things to me, and he's going to help me get Malc transferred to the psych hospital in La Paz. I've been thinking about making Mexico my permanent home for a couple of years now. I got my permanent residence card last year. This situation has been decided for me. Once I get Malcolm settled in La Paz, I'll get my place in Milwaukee on the market and move to Mexico permanently."

Callum waited in an interview room while Julia brought his brother out to talk. She stayed in the room while the brothers spoke. Callum made a list of the additional items Malcolm wanted to take with him the following day. They spoke for several minutes about more personal things. At one point, Malcolm reached out for Callum's hand and his reassurance. Julia felt the pathos of the situation keenly.

As she tidied her desk before leaving for the night, Julia felt as though she'd been on an emotional roller coaster. All she wanted was to collapse on her couch with a glass or two of wine. She had a partial bottle of Merlot in her cupboard. It was calling her.

Cooking was not something she wanted to face that evening, so she picked up two pork tamales from a street vendor on her way home. Forty minutes after leaving the station, she was sprawled on her tiny couch in shorts and a tank top, hair loose, a glass of wine in hand, when her cell rang.

"Bueno," she answered using the typical Mexican greeting.

"Julia, it's Mateo.

Chapter Sixty-Eight – Present Day

"Are you available for dinner with me tonight?" Mateo's resonant voice invoked a warm glow in Julia's chest. She smiled.

"Yes and no," she said. "I'd very much like to see you, but I've already eaten. Would you consider a tamale and some wine dinner?"

Thirty minutes later, Mateo arrived at Julia's casita with a bottle of wine. Julia had changed again and was now clad in a blouse and skirt. She'd also tidied her tiny living space, though in reality, it was never very untidy.

Julia poured the last of her Merlot into a glass for her guest and plated the one remaining tamale. She made a joke about her fine cuisine, and the two fell into a comfortable conversation as Mateo quickly polished off the tamale. The first topic, understandably, was the outcome of Malcolm's hearing. Julia mentioned Malcolm's confession, such as it was. Mateo simply nodded, then said he wasn't surprised.

"In some part of his brain, he knows what he did and that it was wrong. Admitting it is a good sign for his mental stability. If you remember, I said that he was plagued by the cognitive dissonance caused by his inability to admit what he'd done."

Once the hearing had been dissected, Mateo turned their conversation to something more personal. "This has been my favorite psych eval in years, maybe ever," he said as a lead-in. "That is down to meeting you. I have very much enjoyed getting to know you, Julia.

I hope we can continue to stay connected. If that is something you'd like, of course."

The warm spot in Julia's chest grew. "I'd like that."

They talked for hours. Julia felt more comfortable with Mateo than she'd felt with a man, perhaps ever. Romantic liaisons for Julia generally leaned more toward hook-ups than relationships, especially during her years at university. Since getting her master's degree, her focus had been career advancement.

Ricardo was the only consistent man in her life for the past several years. But theirs was a working relationship. This man before her, presented a new option. He didn't live in San Amaro. He wasn't in the police force. She liked him, and he admitted he liked her too. She was definitely interested in seeing where things with him might go.

In her honest and forthright manner, she said all these things to Mateo. In turn, he talked about his past with the same frankness. At midnight, they parted company. Julia walked with him to his car. Their first kiss was a sweet and lingering goodbye.

The warmth in Julia's chest continued to grow.

"Hey, Lucy, you're looking happy today. Are you feeling better about the way the case was resolved?" Ricardo said as Julia entered the war room at eight the next morning. Then, watching her more closely, he went on. "Or is this glow I see the result of your new boyfriend?"

"He's not my boyfriend, not that it's any of your concern, Ricky," Julia emphasized his moniker and flashed him a smile. "Don't make it weird. He's a guy and he's a friend. He also lives on the other side of Baja. Now, let's get this place back to being a conference room.

By late afternoon, they had boxed up and catalogued all their evidence and investigation reports. Ricardo was hauling the file boxes to their records storage room when Julia said she had a few phone calls she wanted to make as part of the close-out.

"Hello, Mr. Walker. This is Detective Sergeant Garcia. I wanted to let you know that the case of the remains found in your cistern has been resolved." She went on to let him know that the guilty party was apprehended and charged. She didn't provide any other details, and he didn't ask for any.

"Are you settling into your new home?" she asked. The man rambled on about the work he'd had done on the property, meeting his neighbors, and appeared ready to launch into a new topic when Julia deftly cut him off, saying she was happy he was enjoying his new life here in Baja and ended the call.

Her next call imparted much the same information she'd given Abe Walker. To Mona Davenport, Julia provided a few additional details. She wanted Mona to know that her friend's killer was incarcerated. She didn't see the need to mention Malcolm's mental incapacity to stand trial. Mona was very appreciative of the information.

Her final call was not related to the case. "Hi Stella, it's Julia. We finally solved the case, so I'm more available now, if you and Pippa need me for anything." They talked for several minutes while Stella updated Julia about their progress in working with the group in Tijuana aimed at reducing human trafficking. They made a date for dinner a few days hence.

Ricardo returned from the records room as Julia was hanging up from her last call. "Can I buy you a beer to celebrate the end of the case?" she asked.

"Absolutely," Ricardo said enthusiastically. "How about including Vicente, too. His contribution was pretty dammed important to our success."

Julia made a show of checking her purse to ensure she had enough money for three beers. When she looked up at Ricardo, he was grinning at her. "Nice try, Lucy. You can afford the first round."

"The second round is on you, Ricky." They laughed amicably.

If you enjoyed Woman in the Cistern, don't miss the next book in the San Amaro series, Death in the Den. And if this is your first time reading a San Amaro mystery, be sure to check out Death in the Baja and Death in the Kitchen, the first two books in the series.

Go to MarnieJRoss.com and subscribe to follow the writing process.

Acknowledgments

I owe huge to thanks my beta readers Linda Wiggins, Cal Whedbee, and Lisbeth Vincent for their insightful feedback as this book took shape, and Tricia Sikes, my wonderful wife, who helped me in more ways than I can possibly list.

About the Author

Marnie Ross is an expatriated dual citizen of Canada and the United States, now living permanently in San Felipe, Baja, Mexico, with her wife, two small rescued dogs, and two rescued cats.

Her passion for her adopted home and murder mysteries is the impetus behind the San Amaro Mystery series. If you want to learn more about Baja living and being an expat in Mexico while enjoying a gripping murder mystery, please sign up at ***marniejross.com***, and experience the adventure.

I always love hearing from my readers, so please don't hesitate to contact me at **marnie@marniejross.com**.

www.ingramcontent.com/pod-product-compliance
Lightning Source LLC
Chambersburg PA
CBHW031945260626
47157CB00017B/2653

* 9 7 9 8 9 9 4 4 5 6 5 0 7 *